Trek
For The
Cross

JADE CROSS TRILOGY

HAROLD W. WEIST

ISBN: 978-1-64314-882-3 (Paperback)
        978-1-64314-883-0 (Hardback)
        978-1-64314-884-7 (E-book)

Library of Congress Control Number: 2023919433

AuthorsPress
California, USA
www.authorspress.com

THE JADE CROSS TRILOGY

JADE CROSS BOOK 1: TREK FOR THE CROSS

AT THE END OF the Sixteenth Century in Dai Viet, what was recently known as North Viet Nam, a devotee to the secret No Name Society began an assignment to receive what would take him to China for the No Name Society. The devotee, Troung Van Ba began, the perilous trek to receive the Jade Cross from a Chinese Master Cutter, a Mr. Hu, along with a secret document related to the Chinese intentions for Dai Viet, to invade or not to. Along the way there were sub hamlets where he would receive an update on the safety issues along his route. At one he was assigned a young, beautiful, 16, years old guide, Tran Thi Mot, which found both taking an immediate dislike for each other. She was assigned to Van Ba as the route had been changed, and he would never choose to work with a woman, A Vietnamese Man thing.

In addition to enduring many hardships during the trek, robbers, murderers, and anti No Name enemies wanting the icon for themselves, were encountered, and battles were fought. Once the Jade Cross was obtained, they were joined along the way by two allies. Many hardships were encountered until the icon was placed into the hand of the No Name Leader, Nguyen Hai. During the trek love evolved between the two protagonists. Van Ba and Mot could not have known that their trek and acquiring the Jade Cross would spur an adventure in the twentieth century, beginning and ending in Vietnam.

JADE CROSS BOOK 2: BEFORE THE ADVENTURE

Master Gunnery Sergeant Travis Tolbane, USMC (Ret.) had served in Vietnam twice during the conflict. He and his interpreter, Nguyen Ba had been on several operations during his first tour. He was lucky to have had Ba assigned to him on his second tour also. They became fast friends, being bonded for life due to several incidents during military operations.

After one miserable operation during cold and driving monsoon rains Tolbane caught a thief, a rouge Marine Private, attempting to steal merchandise from a mini PX situated in a con-ex box at a military enclave on the combat Base at Chu Lai, Republic of Viet Nam. The thief cursed Tolbane, swearing revenge on him for pushing his face into mud. Tolbane had not the least idea that this thief would be his bane during his after-military life, even costing him his first true love.

Tolbane had settled in a small Tennessee town called Mount Juliet, Tennessee. He found a house there and a job as a mall security manager in Nashville. The thief had become the overall boss of several smash and grab gangs in Middle Tennessee area and was headquartered in Nashville. The thief finding out that his sworn enemy, Travis Tolbane was the mall security manager at a mall, he engineered, along with his secretary and lover, Soapy, havoc that affected Tolbane, his friend, Detective Parnell, who had served with Tolbane in Vietnam on a couple of patrols, and mall employees, from a blotched fake shooting to kidnaping and murder, and taking the life of Tolbane's love.

Neither Travis Tolbane nor his friend, Sgt. Parnell could know that after the thief was taken down, their' friendship would later lead to an adventure that began on a patrol in Vietnam in mid-1966 near Hoi An City and ended with the taking down of a vicious Vietnamese Piquerist, who had formed a bogus No Name Cult in the States and believed he was the reincarnation of an ancient, adored Vietnamese General. He had a hatred for Tolbane and his live in Vietnamese lover, the beautiful Mai, and whole incident would climax in Vietnam.

JADE CROSS BOOK 3: THE JADE CROSS

Going home from his job as the Mall Security Manager at Perkins Mall in Nashville, Tennessee, for the day, Travis Tolbane, Retired Master Gunnery Sergeant, USMC, was ambushed by Vietnamese thugs. It was a close call and he was lucky that Metro Police was close at hand. Then shortly after that on the same night he discovered his friend and former interpreter, Ba, had been murdered by a horrendous method known as, Death from a Thousand Cuts, and was staked out like a cross on his kitchen floor.

Various information and incidents led the group, now four, with a Vietnamese Priest, that had been targeted also, joined them in believing the attacks stemmed from a Marine Patrol in 1966 in which Tolbane and Parnell were a part of in which a bejeweled Jade Cross was found and reburied. They also realized the incidents were in a mad Masked Man's CAUSE, who thought he was the reincarnation of Tran Hung Dao, a famous Vietnamese General from the end of the 13th Century and stilled revered, which was a drive to recover an iconic jeweled Jade Cross, take the beautiful Mai for his lover, kill her lover and friends that he hated with a passion, and reunite all of Viet Nam under his power, with he and Mai ruling beside him, along with his bogus No Name Society doing the dirty work.

Tolbane's friend Sgt. Parnell of the Nashville Metropolitan Police Department (MNPD) and Tolbane's Vietnamese lover, Mai, step-sister to Ba, received several threats and attempts on their physical wellbeing over a several-day period. They then learned another previous non-active duty Marine acquaintance was brutalized in the same manner as had Ba.

After a friend of Mai's was brutally beaten and raped the four tracked and followed the mad Masked Man to Hawaii and, Hong Kong where he had left a trail of blood, and finally to Hoi An City in the Democratic Republic of Viet Nam, where he continued to spill blood.

Their quest for the Jade Cross and putting an end to the murderous, piquerist, Masked Man would be aided by a powerful Vietnamese ally, who was once Tolbane's prisoner during the Vietnamese Conflict. Will the four friends find a real No Name Society, and along with their ally succeed in stopping the Masked Man's CAUSE and finding the precious, jeweled Jade Cross, or will Viet Nam be their ultimate fate.

There needs not a great soul to make a Hero, there needs a god-created soul which will be true to its origin.

The guise in which the Hero performs his function is not determined by the fact of his existence. The variety of shapes in which this essential Hero-stuff appears, results from the need of the world into which it comes. Hero can be Poet, Prophet, King, Priest, or what you will, according to the kind of world he finds himself born in to.

From
Carlyle's Theory of the Hero
H. Lehman

PROLOGE

TOWARD THE END OF the Sixteenth Century, the late 1500s, in what became North Vietnam in a later century, Troung Van Ba, was a young and, bold adventurer who became noticed by the leader, Nguyen Hai, of an organization named the No Name that began as a religious and semi-terrorist one, and morphed into a protector of the people. He had fought in skirmishes against bandits attacking defenseless sub-hamlets and served in putting down a rebellion in a large hamlet complex and performed well at each assigned task. He became one of a few of Nguyen Hai's Favorites and most trusted warriors.

The people of the sub-hamlets he championed were very poor peasants, having very little belongings and sometimes they even lacked enough food, sometimes maybe even going as much as two days without. The bandits would steal whatever they could haul away, even went so far as to rape the women, young to old, even beat the elders as well as the young. The bandits could care less as to age, and sometimes even the gender of their victims. The bandits would even murder for no apparent reason, any whim would be satisfied.

Van Ba had been lucky enough to have been rescued as a 5-year-old child by a man of some means. The man, Ngo Doan, was a retired Martial Arts master who came across three bandits in the process of ambushing, robbing and murdering a man and a woman who had a small child with them, Van Ba's mother and father. The child was trying beat on the bandits to help protect his parents. One of the bandits slapped the child in the head knocking him down, but the child jumped back up to hit at the robbers again. Doan tore into them in a fury, killing all three instantly with various martial arts moves.

The child, Troung Van Ba, was picked up in the stranger's arms and hugged close as he whaled and cried over the loss of his mother and father. Doan comforted him and fell in love with the little tyke immediately and, with no time lapse saw a potential in the child, so, he decided he would care for the child and train him so he would not be as defenseless as his father, and to champion and protect those in need. This was not something unusual for Doan. He was known to all as to be a kind and considerate, and passionate man who never hesitated to aid those in the right or in need.

Doan had a beautiful and loving concubine, ten years younger than himself, who not only served as his lover, but cooked, cleaned, and performed whatever ever task Doan need her to do, and she was happy to comply with his every wish and sexual desire. Being childless, she welcomed the tyke, Troung Van Ba, as her own and vowed to raise him to be an honest person and to respect and protect all others also.

Tran Thi Tam had some martial arts skill also, as Doan had taught her to be self-reliant and have the ability to defend herself. Throughout his growing years Van Ba was loved by both and he returned the love to his foster parents ten-fold.

Starting at a very young age he learned to respect his ancestors, was trained not only in martial arts, but in the art of knife fighting, as long knives, cudgels, and swords were the only weapons of the time. As he aged, he toiled in his foster father's fields along with other workers during the day and having his martial arts training in the evenings with his foster-parents which became more technical and intense incrementally through the years. When it was time to sleep at night he would not only sleep like a rock from the day's exertion, but he would be dreamless because of his exhaustion. One morning Doan woke him at the early hour as he usually did. Doan told Van Ba that he could sleep longer that morning as he would not be working the fields that day, and the two would talk later.

After waking again Van Ba went outside, took care of his body urges, threw water on his face, wiped it as dry as his hands could, and went into the kitchen where Doan and Tam were drinking hot tea and conversing in low tones, nearly a whisper. He thought that was a very odd thing for them to do. He wasn't used to their whispering. When he sat down Tam arose and poured a cup of hot tea for the young man and served him a bowl of rice and some bread she had baked early that morning, and patting him on the head. After he'd eaten his fill his foster father decided it was time and informed Van Ba of the situation.

"You have been an upright, loyal, and obedient son, an incredible youngster, obeying Tam and I, working hard in the fields, training with a tireless vigor and you are now past the age of youth. You have become of age and now you're now a man that I see sitting before me. It is time for you to leave the fold and meet the challenges of life as each man must do, and to make you're mark on the world. I will now explain why I've trained you as hard and as thorough I have. First, do you have any questions of me right now?"

"No father I haven't any questions now because I have no idea about what I should question you in regards to."

"You are intelligent to answer me in this manner. You're very wise for your age. Let me enlighten you. When I came upon the scene I saw you trying to fight those men who were robbing and murdering your parents. I knew then that you were special, and you could be a game changer for the poor people who suffer from those who would take advantage of them. They need someone skilled in the arts to protect or to avenge them. You are that man, Troung Van Ba. I have chosen, and trained you to fight evil and succeed."

Continuing Doan said, "Sadly, today is your last day with us. Two men will come for you later this morning. You will take your possessions and go with them. They will teach you how to find and defeat the disgusting asses that terrify, rob, and rape, and murder the peasants. You will not question them. You will just follow their instructions to the hilt. You will face many perils on this journey. You will have many fights, and you may have to kill to destroy the evil ones, or even be killed yourself. Those you kill will be no different than the ones who killed your parents. You must feel absolutely no remorse for them. They will die doing the evil they chose to do at your' hands. Your martial arts skill and your knife fighting will be tested over and over, but you are a winner, you will prevail. Now, are there any questions my son?"

"Leave here! Leave yours and Tam's love for a kind of life like that? Do you not love me?"

"MY son. Tam and I love you dearly and we will miss you every moment until we are with our ancestors. Even then our love for you will never die. Tam and I have pained over this day for years. This is your destiny. I knew it the first time I saw you attempting to save your' parents. You will always be the peoples champion and respected by all except the evil ones who will fear you. But first you must learn how to apply your skills to defeat them. The two men coming here today will be your tutors, they will teach you, but you will have to learn what they teach."

"If this is my destiny, then it must be my future, my life. But I still don't understand. I don't want to leave you two. I have served you as any son would. I've toiled and trained as hard as I could for you, my father, and obeyed you my mother. I never realized that there was a reason for my training and it would be my life. I will always hold you and Mom in my heart. If I should survive this life I'm destined to I will always thank you for giving me the skills to survive.

A year later Van Ba, after more rigorous training and learning, and the two men who were his mentors, Trich Le and Nguyen Bon, had camped and slept on a little rise overlooking the large sub-hamlet of Do Dia #3. It was large enough to have a small market where the three had bought some dry rice, bread and fresh tea leaves. Just as they were finishing their morning fare one of the men, Bon, was looking towards the sub-hamlet, enjoying the sight of the area in the early light before the sun rose. He turned his head to the right looking at the road leading into the sub-hamlet. He immediately hushed the others and pointed a way up the road. Van Ba could see five scroungy, dirty looking individuals, most likely bandits, carrying bags of what was probably booty, slowly heading toward the sub hamlet. He could see their knives. That could mean only one thing. They were on the way to Do Dia #3 to rob, rape and murder again.

The three lay down quickly in a prone position to keep out of sight, huddled and talked of what strategy they would use to attack the bandits. Over the past year they had used various rouses to confront the evil ones. The one that was decided on was, proven to work time after time. For two of them to confront the five on the road while the third one snuck up behind them. Van Ba had always been the one to sneak up and attack from behind. This time the leader Trick Le informed Van Ba that he, Van Ba, and Nguyen Bon would meet the five in front of the sub hamlet while he attacked from the rear.

"Van Ba," It's time for you to step up and demonstrate to us that our training of you has not been in vain, and has taken root. I feel that you are the best I've ever trained. I need you now to show me that I'm not wrong about you."

"Remember, don't attack them until I'm in place, but defend yourself if they attack you. Your long knives must speak for you both today. The bandits must go to their ancestors this very day and we to ours on another day. Always remember, don't anticipate that they have no fighting skills. Some bandits have had some fight training, have some skills, and have had fighting experience. Let your natural instincts kick in and be your guide. Good luck my friends. Now let us sneak into our positions."

Bent over at the waist, Van Ba and Bon quickly moved down the slope where they couldn't be seen by the five and made their way to the entrance to the sub hamlet to seem like they came from the sub hamlet, turned and began walking towards the scroungy five, they moved with their shoulders rolled back, their statures erect and they strode with confidence towards the bandits.

As the five closed the distance to the duo the five stopped, dropped their bags, drew out their long knives, and one of them stepped forward. He announced, "My name is Nguyen Nghia and I am this gang's leader. You two must step aside quickly so we may enter the sub-hamlet in a peaceful manner."

Van Ba assumed the lead as he had been assigned, took two steps toward him, stared and stated. "You scallywags do not look like anyone in this sub-hamlet in his right mind would care to have you enter their domicile! In fact, you five look pretty damn stinky and scroungy to me. Have you been wallowing with the pigs?"

"Look behind me you most unworthy and lowlife one. We are five experienced fighters and you are only two insolent and insignificant idiots, unworthy cock roaches thinking that you are great fighters and protectors of the lowly peasants in this sub-hamlet. Hah! Hah! Ha! Move your asses aside now and we will spare you your lives, or if you prefer, you will meet your ancestors where you stand!"

Van Ba and Bon just laughed at him, drew their long knives, stood their ground and just smiled back and laughed some more. Bon replied, "There is also a chance that it maybe it will be you five who go to the ancestor meeting this day. Did you ever think of that? Maybe your ancestors won't want you either?"

The comment angered him and just as Nguyen Nghia was about to give his gang the order to attack Trich Le had silently moved into the five's rear and quickly took out two of the bandits with his long knife. As the other three turned to see what the commotion was, Van Ba and Bon attacked making short work of two bandits with Nguyen Nghia, dropping his long knife, being shocked just stood there, a dumbfounded soul.

"Well, just don't stand there like a dumb cock roach Van Ba stated. Sit down on your filthy ass, cross your ankles, and place your hands-on top of your head and make sure you keep your mouth shut unless your being spoken to. You got that cock roach?" Looking with horror at his captors, Nguyen Nghia complied with the instructions. As he sat down the front of his pajama bottoms suddenly became wet and smelly. He was scared for his life.

Van Ba watched the prisoner as the other two gathered the long knives from the four bodies, and opened the bags. The bags contained common household items, such as cooking pots, some stale bread and some rice, and etc., and clothing. By now several sub-hamlet members came out to watch what was happening. They were very curious as to who these saviors of their people were. Finely one of them Spoke up.

"I'm the Do Dia #3 Sub-Hamlet Chief, Bui Van Tam. Who are you? Do you mean us suffering too?

Trich Le spoke up. "I am Trich Le. This man is Nguyen Bon, and the young man is Troung Van Ba. I'll answer one question at a time. First, we are wonderers who have dedicated ourselves to seek out bandits, rapists, and murderers to defeat them and to protect our country's men and women and children. All three of us were victims of sorts at one time or another and we want no one to suffer the things we have had to suffer during our lifetime."

"Now to your second question. We mean neither you nor your people any harm what so ever. One thing we do is give whatever loot we take from bandits to the sub-hamlet people. All this booty is yours to distribute among the peasants. That includes the five long knives. The only condition we ask is that you must bury the bodies for us."

The Chief queried, "If you are being truthful about this, what can we do for you in return besides burying the bodies, for we are grateful for your actions. We had heard these five were headed our way and had no idea how to protect our women and children, keeping them safe from harm. Being a poor sub-hamlet, we have little to give, but we will grant you anything that we are able to, Bui replied.

"Honorable Chief Bui, we would only ask, of you, for a hot meal, and a sheltered place to sleep tonight, and if it's at all possible, a little dry rice and fresh bread to take with us in the morning," Trich replied. "We will also show any five men you chose a little about using the scum's long knives to protect your people. Even then your defense should be by ruse and attack as we did here. Also train your other men to attack the bandits with their tools or sticks at the same time to overwhelm the evil ones. Usually, bandits try to stay from the places that defends its selves."

"Your need for this night is granted and we will forever be in your debt."

The three fighters were led into the sub hamlet and received gratitude from the peasants as they were guided to a deserted hovel. Chief Bui informed them food would be brought to them and they were welcome to stay in the hovel as long as they desired. The feasted that night, spent the next day training five men as best as they could. The day after that they left the sub-hamlet early morning with rice and freshly baked bread before the peasants awoke.

They traveled for two and a half days before arriving at a large populated area. Trich led them to a large house like structure where they were greeted by two servants who served them tea and bread. After serving the tea one of the servants left the room and returned with a very distinguished gentleman. Van Ba wondered if the man was a Mandarin. He had never seen a man wearing such a plush Long gown before.

Van Ba was introduced to the man, Nguyen Hai, the leader of the No Name. Van Ba bowed at the waist with his palms pressed together in front of his face. He did not understand why he was being introduced to such a warrior and leader of the people's defense against the people's enemies. He was awed and at a loss for words. Not really knowing how to react to this meeting he managed to utter a few words. "This is an honor for such an unworthy one as I."

Nguyen Hai motioned for Van Ba to stand erect. "You have no reason to bow to me. I'm no greater than any other man, nor are you. I know you must wonder why you've been brought here. I too wonder why," Nguyen Hai stated looking at Trich Le.

"Oh, honorable one I have been training this young man for a good year and I cannot praise him highly enough. I think once we discuss his accomplishments I think you will want him to be a No Name fighter for justice. Troung Van Ba is a better fighter than most of your men. He's obedient, respectful, loyal, and has been well trained in martial arts, knife fighting by Ngo Doan, and he uses his brain. His long knife has sent many bandits to their ancestors quickly. He can think and act quickly to any situation. I think he would be an asset to your operations."

Nguyen Hai looked up and down at Van Ba for a full five minutes, and then enquired of him. "Young man, what do you think about the last year of hardships and adventures you have been in throughout the past year?"

Van Ba thought for a moment then began, "As my foster father told me, I was destined and raised to protect the defenseless and to put down the evil ones where I find them. This has been ingrained in me during all the hard work and training I've endured since I was rescued by Ngo Doan as I watched my parents murdered. I now wish to make this kind of life my destiny, my fate, and let life take me where my fate awaits."

"Well-spoken young man." Nguyen Hai continued after a short pause. "Our organization always needs good young men with your talents and your' tenacity. You need to know that everyone in our organization swears to keep the No Name sacred and never reveal its secrets, no matter what duress they suffer under or die to keep."

"This humble and not worthy one understands the consequences of any betrayal to the No Name, my honorable one," Van Ba answered. "I pledge my life to the No Name, and I will be the best man I am able to be and I will obey your orders to the death."

"Welcome to the No Name Troung Van Ba. Now learn this. You will never again use the words honorable, unworthy, and any other similar ones in my presence again. We are the same, there's no difference between us. We are all flesh and blood, and we bleed the same. We are all destined to return to the dust from which we came. It is preordained for each of us from birth. Now, one of my aides will show you your quarters and provide a good meal. Tomorrow," looking Van Ba in the eyes he said, "you will be tested for a couple of days so we may assess your skills and abilities allowing us to assign you tasks that is within your abilities to handle." Nguyen Hai smiled at Van Ba, called an aide and left the room. Trich Le and Nguyen Bon followed as an aide led Van Ba out to a small hovel and introduced him to a trainer. They said their good byes to him and were gone.

Three days later Nguyen Hai summoned Van Ba to the same room he had arrived at. "Young man, all of our testers were impressed with you in your tests. You have great skills and presence for one so young. They feel you will be able to take on the most difficult tasks with ease. You are now a member of the No Name."

Van Ba was elated. "Thank you! When do I start my first assignment?"

"Patience is a virtue my young man. Something that youth must acquire during their journey throughout their life time. You must learn to bide your time. As soon as an event arises worthy of your capability you will be briefed and sent on your way, alone. Until then, you need to relax and enjoy the easy life, but still train each day. I might add, not that it would interest any young man like you, but in the nearby sub-hamlet there are some very young and pretty girls, and not nearly enough young men to go around. Now be on your way and enjoy."

With a big smile on his face from the mention of pretty young girls, Van Ba stated, "I thank you again Nguyen Hai. I will never fail you. I'm your servant until death." He left with a spring in his step and kept his promise all of his life.

It was in this sub-hamlet, Bin Sanh #1 that he met his future wife.

CHAPTER 1

VIET NAM IS A country bordering on the west side of the South China Sea, basically East of Cambodia and Laos and abutting China in its Northwestern area. Its people like to say that, "Viet Nam is shaped like an S." When looking at its position on a map it does indeed give the impression of an elongated "S". Below Ho Chi Minh City, formerly called Sai Gon, is The Mekong river and its delta areas. From above Ho Chi Minh City going generally north is the Annamite Range extending to what was the Demilitarized Zone, which lay between the north and south areas demarcated during the Geneva Peace Accord of 1954.

From the DMZ[1] area the Annamite Cordillera takes up most of the northern area. The South has coastal lowlands inundated with rice paddies, farm lands, small hedge rows and large populated areas. Between the coastal lowlands is a piedmont stretching to the Annamite Range. There are many jungle areas too. The yearly temperatures will range from 63 to 82 degrees in the north and averages around 80

---

[1]   De-Militarized Zone.

degrees in the South with up to 79 inches of rainfall during monsoon season.

The recorded history of Viet Nam begins about 208 BC in Chinese annals when a turncoat Chinese General, Trieu Da, conquered the Viet People of Au Lac, in the Northern mountain area. The Viet were of Mongolian origin having migrated south. General Trieu Da then proclaimed himself the 'Emperor' of "Nam Viet," the land of Viet South. This land reached to the area of Tourane, presently the city of Da Nang. A century later this area was annexed by the Chinese Empire and they called the Viets, 'Yueh'.

From the 13th Century on the Vietnamese Language was written in variant Chinese Characters, each character representing one word, based on the Classical Chinese, but supplemented with characters developed in Viet Nam to represent native Vietnamese words which has varying tones. Later, in the 13th Century a first and second Mongol invasions were thwarted by General Tran Hung Dao. General Tran Hung Dao left a book describing how to make booby traps such as Punji Pits and etc., and also how to conduct Guerilla Warfare, which was a new concept at the time to the area. The book is kept protected in today's time in Hanoi and its contents were by General Vo Nguyen Giap against the French and later the American and free world forces in a protracted conflict.

In1527 Portuguese Christian Missions used the Latin alphabet to transcribe the Vietnamese Language for teaching purposes. This led to the development of the modern-day Vietnamese alphabet by a French Jesuit Priest, Alexander de Rhodes. Rhodes worked in Viet Nam from 1624 to 1644. He also built on to existing Portuguese/Vietnamese dictionaries.

The Viet, over later centuries had wars with the Chinese, and neighboring Cambodia. They also had many traders and enclaves established at various times by the French, Dutch, English, Spanish (for 400 years), and the Portuguese. They called Viet Nam "Cochin China" after a Chinese character for Viet Nam to separate it from another colony named Cochin. During the French colonization, the French called the southern end of Viet Nam "Cochinchina," the center "Annam" and the Northern portion "Tonkin, hence Indo-china."

Prior to the Second World War the French controlled Viet Nam and it was referred to as French Indo-China. With the expansion of the Japanese Far East Co-Prosperity Sphere Japan had taken over Viet Nam, allowed the Vichy French to continue administering the country, and the Viet organized the Viet Minh to combat the Japanese in a guerilla type warfare. After the Surrender of the Japanese the French once again took hold of Viet Nam. The Viet Minh continued their guerilla warfare with the French. The French were finally defeated in 1954 at the battle of Dien Bien Phu.

After the defeat of the French, the country was divided into North and South Viet Nam by a demilitarized zone by the Geneva Accords of 1954. According to the pact, elections were to be held to unite the two sections into one country with the two areas holding a National Election. The North portion was mainly Socialist/Communist, and the South eventually became a Republic. Nearly one million Catholics migrated South and the North would only allow about one hundred twenty thousand or so Viet Minh and sympathizers to come north, leaving many more to remain in the south as future cadre and infiltrate the South's infrastructures and etc.

Later, after the South decided not to hold a national election between the two factions the North started supporting rebel factions in South Viet Nam and organized the National Liberation Front (NLF). The rebels, Viet Communists, were named Viet Cong[2] by the South's President Diem. Viet Cong was actually an insult by then Premiere Diem, meaning Red Viet. Then the North started to send troops to The South. In the 60's, U.S. President Kennedy began sending advisers to South Viet Nam. Then in 1965, U. S. President Johnson sent troops to assist the South after the Ton Kin incident. The Americans left in 1972. In 1975 the North sent large forces sweeping into the South capturing the Republic. This united the country under Communist rule.

In 1535 Antonio Da Faria, a Portuguese Catholic Missionary, found a nice site for a harbor at Fai Fo, (Ancient Chinese trade city, today Hoi An City), south of Tourane (Da Nang). The Portuguese wanted to make Fai Fo a major enclave and port, but it didn't work out. While Da Faria was in Faifo he developed a large following; converting a lot of the people to Christianity. It was rumored that he also developed a secret cult like society. The religion of the cult was based on Catholicism and had no name to speak of, hence it was called the "No Name Society."

After Da Faria left the country a very powerful mandarin, Nguyen Hai, became the cult leader and proceeded to build into it an ultimate secret cult society, moved its operation to the North, and it was still called the No Name, which would propagate throughout Viet Nam, even today. Originally, the main function of this cult was to help the poor farmers and laborers attain a better way of life and to punish those who would take advantage of the farmers and laborers, and reunite all of Vietnam as one. As the cult evolved, murder,

---

[2]   Red Viet

kidnapping and robbery became the instruments to obtain not only wealth for the cult, but it was against those who were shown to be against the people and sided at times with the Chinese, and with a share of the wealth going to needy peasants.

Many of the Viet Mandarins in areas attempted to penetrate the cult's secrecy by having their agents infiltrate the cult's rank and file and gather information to help put it down. These attempts were never successful. The agent's bodies would be found later, tortured to death by what the Asians called the "Death of a thousand cuts." Eventually the No Name would no longer commit crimes and remained for the good of the people."

It is whispered that the cult has survived many conflicts through its covertness. Generations of members would pass on the secrets of the cult from father to son and were active behind the scenes in the Viet Minh's struggle with the invading Japanese and later with the Viet Cong against the Americans and her allies, and many of them supported the South.

Part of its legend relates that this cult society guarded something very valuable, the likes of which had never been seen. In 1575, Troung Van Ba, an agent of Nguyen Hai, lived in a sub hamlet a little South and West of Hanoi. One Day Nguyen Hai came to Van Ba's hovel to visit and while there Van Ba was given a secret mission to cross into China to find out if China had plans to invade because of political tensions in the region and in addition to obtain a priceless package for the No Name from a Chinese artisan. Troung was selected because he was fluent in Chinese dialects and his loyalty to Nguyen Hai could not be questioned, as he had proven this loyalty many times and in many ways over the years. He was now faced with a very hazardous foot journey through the Annamite Mountain Range. Besides the worry of obtaining food and water, there were the threat of bandits, murderers, and Chinese troops along what passed as roads; just mere paths and was of great concern to him.

Van Ba collected what information he could on the areas he must trod through on foot and made elaborate plans for his trip. Nguyen Hai had provided contact names and routes for his trip and collection efforts. He needed to know first where to find loyalists to the cause along the way who could provide any needed food, clothing, shelter, and or protection during his trek and information on avoiding enemies and criminals. He also had to consider the sun, the heat, the cold, the wind, the rain, sleeping without shelter at times and could not discount any snows that could hinder his progress.

After a week of collecting all the information he could, he began his preparation by modifying his clothing. The first modification was to sew secret pockets into the inside of his tunic to hold the various documents of introduction to his main Chinese contact, those agents which gave travel routes, hamlets, sub hamlets, allies, and lesser contacts inside China and etc. Two pockets would contain sharpened knives for protection and as tools for cutting firewood or any other use. For colder weather he made some foot socks, two extra trousers and two tunics a little larger than his size so that they would fit over his every day Clothes. Next was a two-blanket roll into which he could place rice, vegetables, bread, nuoc mam sauce, extra clothes, a small cooking pot and several pairs of bootie like socks, and two pair of sandals.

Van Ba would loop the blanket roll over one arm and then over his head. He believed he would look like any wanderer the people along the way would see. In addition to his conical hat, he made a bandana he could place on his head under his conical hat and also to cover his ears in the cold. He felt he was well prepared and ready for the physical part of the trip.

The next step was to review his travel information and draft a map showing his route, travel stops, and areas to avoid. He would have to conceal the map and papers on his person in a manner that it would not easily be found. The average wonderer would never have a map. He decided also if any one confronted him it might be in his best interests to pretend to be like an ignorant peasant, dumb, and not knowing where he was going.

Now is the time for a last sexual visit, and eat some good cooking with his secret girlfriend, Nguyen Thi Tranh, for a day or two, then have a good, one day's rest. She was still very good looking for her middle age. She lived alone as she had been widowed as a young wife when her older husband was killed by bandits. She never remarried because she could find no man worthy of her charms although she had had a couple of affairs that didn't turn out well. She was happy when she was with him and she felt she would marry Van Ba if he ever asked her as he was the only man, she felt that was worthy of her.

Though he adored her, he knew he could never really love her as sometimes his heart still belonged to his beloved wife who had passed away early in life from a malady he knew nothing about, but he did like Tranh a little more than some of the other women he had before her. Her body was always an extreme delight to him and the way she would always listen to his woes and make him feel like a man as best she could. He would miss, besides the sex, her cooking and domestic skills and hopped he would return and they would couple together once more on occasion.

After seeing his secret girlfriend Tranh for two days of eating, making love and being coddled by Tranh, he felt well satisfied and was at peace with himself. After another day's rest, he took a long nap during the afternoon then stealthily crept from his sub-hamlet well after dark to avoid being seen by the wrong villager. Hopefully they were all sleeping. He had picked up his supplies, slit a hole in the back of his hovel and crept about a half mile down to a meandering creek, followed it about two hundred yards and then circled around to till he came to the main path out of the area and began his long tiresome trek to China.

CHAPTER 2

Troung Van Ba knew he was safe traveling on the main path this time of night. Everyone around any of the sub hamlets he would pass by were farmers and they would be sleeping this time of night because they have to arise early in the morning to tend their fields, paddies, etc., and water buffaloes. After walking about four miles and skirting some sub-hamlets just in case, he walked into a tree line, removed his conical hat, laid down under a tree and slept a dreamless sleep.

When he awoke just after dawn, he placed his conical hat on his head and moved to the path and began his trek once more. He felt he was far enough along the way he could stay on main paths now and safely move through any sub-hamlet or hamlet area without being recognized and continued on at a moderate pace. By noon he had walked through several sub-hamlets and passed many Vietnamese going to their markets or working the fields and paddies.

Many were women with a long pole balanced on one shoulder that had baskets loaded with food or whatever suspended by cords at each end and walking with a quick stride that kept their load balanced and easier to carry. The basket loads were usually fire wood, fish, rice, bread, vegetables, or odd and ends to sell at the market. He would smile and nod to them, being satisfied he was not known to them. Midmorning he bought some fish from one, bread from another and sat by the road and satisfied his hunger.

An hour after eating he found himself in the village's town. He wondered around looking at small houses and huts, making sure that the people saw him as a homeless wonderer. He finely found the Market Place and a small tea shop by the entrance. He went in the tea shop, removed his conical hat and sat at a small table. A young girl about ten years old came out from the family room, bowed, greeted him and asked for his order. He asked for hot tea. The girl went into the rear and a few minutes later returned with a small pot of hot tea and a cup on a tray. She poured him a cup then retreated into the back once more. Looking around and satisfying himself he was alone, Van Ba took out a document that contained a list of villages, hamlets, sub-hamlets and the names of contacts in those locations that had been given to him.

He knew he was in the Binh Tuy Village's built-up area and found the village name on the document and the name of Nguyen Son, the cane maker. This was the person who would feed, shelter him for a day or so, pass on any needed information and put him on the path to his next contact. He felt he was too early to make contact with the man so he bided his time and drank his pot of tea slowly. After a time, he left the tea shop and then he walked into the Market. He strolled through, stopping at vendors to buy bread, dried fish and nuoc mam.[3] He inquired of the venders and shoppers if they knew Nguyen Son the cane maker and how to find him. Finally, one women vendor, about fifty years old, looking about eighty from working long hours in the fields with the sun taking a toll on her

---

[3]   Fermented fish sauce.

body during her whole life, solved the dilemma. She gave him directions to Son's hovel.

Van Ba left the Market and started up the main path looking for a hut with an old man sitting in front of a hovel and carving walking canes. About a hundred feet past the next to last thatched house he found his man. Nguyen Son, growing old and grizzled, his hair a mixture of white with some dark streaking, a shaggy white mustache and a chin beard, and no hair on his cheeks was sitting cross legged in front of his hovel carving a decorative dragon on a cane. He looked up as Troung approached him, wondering what the traveler wanted. Troung greeted the man with a bow and asked, "Hello, are you Nguyen Son the cane maker?" The old man nodded with agreement, still curious as to what the man wanted.

Looking into the old man's eyes the man said, "I am Troung Van Ba, a pilgrim on a quest for the No Name!" Troung then took out a paper of introduction and handed it to Nguyen Son.

The old man satisfied with the prearranged introduction words, read the paper and stated, "I've been expecting you. Come!" With this the old man put down his carving knife and cane, rose and the two entered the hovel. Van Ba being a little taller than the old man removed his conical hat and lowered his head a little in order to enter. The old man pointed to a mat lying at one side of the room told Troung, "Lie here and rest. I'll return later." Nguyen Son then left the hovel. Van Ba lay down on the mat and got as comfortable as you could get on the ground and a mat. All the while he was wondering what the old man was up to, and would it benefit himself. As tired as the trip, so far, had made him, he soon fell into a relaxing sleep, dreaming about his secret girlfriend.

As the sun was disappearing Nguyen Son returned to the hovel, bringing fish, bread and nuoc mam for the two.

This was OK by Van Ba. This way he could keep his own food. They ate in silence while sating themselves. After eating the old man, not knowing where the young man, compared to himself came from, inquired of Troung Van Ba about his journey so far. Van Ba related that so far it had been a safe trip, a lot of walking, and he did not see any one who knew him and it was rather pleasant so far; also. Then Van Ba asked him, "I must ask of you many questions. What is the next leg of my journey? Where will I be going? Is it far? Who will I contact? Will it be one of the persons on my list?"

The old man answered, "Be patient. Tomorrow you can take it easy. Stroll through the market or do anything else you like. Maybe even find a girl to talk to or make a lot of love. Ha! Ha! I'll be gone when you awake. I'll return at nightfall and give you the next stop and contact on your list. You will not go to all of the locations on it. There are some are blind alleys. You will understand all when I return. At the Market place make sure you by extra clothes, blanket, food and cooking utensils, an extra sleeping mat and a bag to carry all. Enjoy tomorrow for you have a harder journey ahead of you. Now have a good night's sleep my friend. There will be days ahead when you won't get much rest." Nguyen Son then spread out another mat, laid down and was soon asleep. Van Ba did the same.

Van Ba slept a lot longer than he usually did. When he awoke, he stretched, felt refreshed, very calm, and glad to be alive. The sun was up and he could feel the warmth that was already creeping into the hovel. It felt good. Then realizing that the old man was not there caused him to feel alone for a while. After a bit, Troung grabbed his conical hat, left the hovel and went back to the tea shop. The same young girl was there. She greeted him with a smile as she had before and served him bread and hot tea at his request. He savored his late breakfast, eating and drinking slowly. The girl came out of the back room heading for the entrance. He called her over to him. He asked her name. "Ngo Thi Mai," she answered. Van Ba told her she was a very pretty girl for being one so young, and he gave her five Dong, (Vietnamese money), and sent her on her way. Later on, after he left the tea shop, he went to the Market area as he had been advised by old Mr. Son.

The market seemed to be a little larger this day. Maybe it just had more vendors than the day before. He strolled around taking his time and talking to shoppers and vendors and enjoying himself there. When he began to tire, he made his purchases from different vendors. A couple changes of clothes, more dried fish, rice, bread, vegetables, nuoc mam, items to cook and eat with, an extra blanket and a large cloth bag with a shoulder strap to carry things. While selecting his purchases he could not keep from wondering what was going on with the old man and what seemed like, to him, changes to his travel plan. He guessed it seemed dumb to follow the old man's instructions without question, but he knew he must do it for the No Name.

He returned to the hovel and placed his purchases in side on top of a mat with what he had bought the day before, beside his blanket roll and then went outside to sit and enjoy the rest of his afternoon. Van Ba dozed off several times and felt at home. He wished he could live this kind of life every day. There was nothing to beat napping whenever one wanted too. He was also wondering where the old man was, what he was up to and when would he return. It was nearly dark so he got up and entered the hovel, ate dried fish and bread. Not having a thing to do, he just lay on the mat and daydreamed about his secret girlfriend again, wished she were sitting on him, and what might happen to him on his trek. Would it be dangerous?

He had not considered this before. If it was to be, he'd face it when it happened.

Just after dark he heard a noise and voices outside and the old man entered the hovel followed by what looked like an old a woman carrying a large bag. Van Ba's eyes got big when he saw she was not an old lady, but a young and pretty one, and he blurted out, "Du Me! (Mother Fucker), who is she and what's she doing here?" The old man just smiled at him. Nguyen Son said to Van Ba, "Say hello to Tran Thi Mot, who is now your travel guide. You two will see a lot of each other during your quest."

Tran Thi Mot moved farther into the room and Troung could see that she was really an older child. Maybe fifteen or sixteen. Could even be seventeen. His temper was about to get the better of him. She looked at him with fire in her eyes and said, "Du Me Nhieu (Mother Fuck you much)!" She used the Vietnamese slang words for people who have sex with their mother at the end of the statement directed at Van Ba. Now he was really livid.

Nguyen Son knew he had an instant problem on his hands. He barked at the two to shut up and quiet down and relax then said to them, "You two must be still and listen to me, or else," as he picked up a heavy cane, "this will quiet you both very quickly." The two stared crossly at each other, then quieted themselves and listened to Son.

"Van Ba," he said, "You must keep the list of places and contacts on your body just in case you should be captured. Don't destroy them. Except for my name and village all the rest are false. Some of the names and places do not exist. If caught you must be very adamant that they are real. Tell the captors that you and your little sister are traveling to those places to find work for the two of you so you can settle down and live a good life. You've been wondering about for three years or so without any family and friends, and living a vagabond's life. Your parents are dead and you two are all you have. You will have plenty time to get your stories straight. I hope you are not caught; on the way back especially."

"You won't like this next thing, but it's a must. Van Ba, Miss Tran Thi Mot will, as I have said, be your guide. She has been to your destination area many times and could travel it blind folded, to and back. She will be the only one who knows where and when to make contact and to whom to make it to. Pointing at his brain with a gnarled finger he said, "She never forgets anything. She has a marvelous brain, and she has a very fast recall. She is the boss of the actual travel. She is older than she looks by a couple of years and she has studied martial arts from the best Monks in China. She's good and she reacts well to situations very quickly. Listen to her when she speaks and stay free and alive. As far as the mission is concerned you are the one in charge. You two must learn to share and to listen to one another as each of you have had many different experiences in your ungrateful lives. All decisions that are made by you two individuals must be as one and must be the right ones. If you do not get along your whole journey will be a huge failure. The No Name needs success in this endeavor, not failure because you two cannot get along."

"Now children, greet each other nicely, lie down on your mats and sleep. You must be gone before the dawn comes."

The children did greet each other in a more friendly way then they lay down on their mats facing away from each other and slept. Van Ba slept soundly as did the girl. Neither of them snored. Well before either kid got a full night's sleep Nguyen Son was shaking and waking them. "Let's go children! Time's a wasting. Get your stuff packed quietly and get ready to leave." The two travelers stretched and yawned then started to pack up their gear. Van Ba was done first so he asked if he could help Mot, but she refused his help. Right at this time she didn't like him, but she must put up with him as well as he must put up with her, for that was her duty.

They said good bye to the old man and he bade them a good quest and exited the hovel. Van Ba and Mot waved and left the old man standing in the darkness and wondering, even though he liked both Troung and Tran, wondering if having those two together was a huge mistake by Nguyen Hai. For the sake of the mission he hoped to hell that was not the case.

When the two were far enough from the old man's area to be heard, Mot told Van Ba, "There will be nights we must sleep close together for warmth. There will be no unwanted touching by you and definitely no sex under any circumstance, do you understand Mister Troung Van Ba? If you don't there will be big trouble. You could end up singing with a very high-pitched voice."

"I have no choice but to abide by your rules. Your body will be safe with me when I'm beside you. I will keep my hands and the other body part away from the places you ask me to. I've already decided for myself that you are not worthy of my touching you anyhow. I have touched many real women and I don't think you qualify as one." He was still steaming about having to have her with him.

"This is what we will face. We'll be going around some small mountains and over others," Mot explained to him. "The journey will be filled with many hazards. I hope you are up to it," as she looked into his eyes. He saw hardness in her eyes and he didn't respond. They continued on their way, a little slower than Van Ba was used too because of the extra gear they carried. Both individuals were ignoring each other, but staying close. After about an hour and a half Mot increased the pace a little. Van Ba, looking down on the path, wondered if she was going to try to tire him out. He's thinking, "What in the world am I doing here with this tough assed young girl? This damn trip is not going as well as I had expected it to. Why am I stuck with this poor excuse for a female? It isn't fair." When he lifted his head, he saw a sub-hamlet ahead and hoped they could get some fresh water and a short rest there.

Arriving there she led Van Ba to a large hovel on the far side of the sub hamlet. She called out her name into the hovel, "It's Mot," and received an answer saying to enter quickly. When the two were in the hovel there was a middle-aged woman cleaning fresh vegetables. Mot spoke quickly to Van Ba. "Neither you nor the woman have a need to know any names. Just be polite to her. She will feed us our next meal and let us know if there are any bandits in the area or places we should avoid. If you need her for anything just call her, Woman!"

With the hovel being larger than most it had a back entrance. The Woman guided them out the back and into the yard. There was a large rectangular table with four chairs around it. The Woman asked them to sit and be quiet. She went inside and returned with a large tea pot with hot tea and cups and served the travelers. She told them that soon the food would be served. She went into the house again.

After the Woman went back inside, Mot leaned towards Van Ba and informed him in a soft and whispered voice that this would their last stop for a few days and on the trail she would do all of their cooking. He only had to gather wood and start the fires as needed. Van Ba smiled at her for the first time since he had met Mot and said, "That's fine with me. A woman is supposed to cook meals for a man! Besides, I'm a great fire maker." Mot had a scowl on her face at that sexist comment.

Then Mot gave him a weird look and began looking around. Everything looked normal to her. She then allowed herself to relax only a little for this duty of hers was a great burden on her as it was to him. She couldn't relax all the way until this was over and she had safely returned to her home and no longer had to put up with this creepy old guy.

Van Ba and Mot sat staring at each other, and mumbling to themselves anew. After a while the Woman brought them each two bowls of food and some bread, and chop sticks. One of the bowls was of rice and the other of boiled vegetables and greens. She refilled their tea cups, told them to call her if they needed anything and she went back inside. The pair then ate silently and greedily till they were full.

As the two finished eating a young man came from the right side of the hovel, looked around, walked up to them and he sat himself at one of the empty chairs. He looked at the two and smiled. "After you two are done eating and drinking tea you will come with me. I'm to take you to a hovel where you will be updated for your trek and you will rest there for the night. It will be the last shelter you will have for a few days. You will be fed rice, tea and bread before you leave in the morning. You will never see me again after you enter the hovel. Someone else is waiting there patiently, just waiting for you two to arrive."

When the meal was finished the three soon left the woman's house without going back inside and giving a, goodbye. The three walked a short distance back the in the direction they had come. Soon the group arrived at their destination. They entered the hovel, one much smaller than the Woman's, and found an old man who was similar in looks to Nguyen Son, even though he looked older, his hair was whiter, but he seemed wiser. He was leaning on a walking stick and welcomed them to his humble abode. He bade the two to pull out their mats, sit on them and be quiet, and they did. The old man had difficulty sitting due to stiffness of his old bones. "Give an old man a moment to sit," he said, "and I will tell you why you are here."

The old man was finally able to sit down and then he seemed to doze off to dream-land and the pair waited patiently giving each other bad looks and mumbling to themselves about the other until he awoke.

CHAPTER 3

THE OLD MAN FINALLY woke and shook his head to clear it. "Please forgive me. I must apologize for my sleepy behavior. It is an old man's weakness. I need another minute." More like five minutes had passed when he finally said, "Troung Van Ba, Tran Thi Mot, since you left the Binh Tuy area, all things have changed. The man you need to meet is no longer in China, so your trek will not be so long. He is now in Viet Nam. It will still be a long way, but shorter than going into China over the worst mountains."

"I have been told he has a very valuable package for you Van Ba; what it is, I have no idea. After receiving the package, you two will return it to Nguyen Hai by a different route, which will be given to you there. It seems that there are those who do not want the package to go to Nguyen Hai and want to use it for their own cause. They are not above robbery, rape, and murder to obtain the package. They have much hate, it's said, for the No Name and Nguyen Hai, and they want revenge for unknown reasons."

Van Ba and Mot looked with surprise at the old man, then at each other each. As they gazed into each other's eyes, something seemed to communicate a newfound trust in each other and a reason for a closeness between them. It gave each one a strange new feeling of dependency upon the other. It was almost as though they were bonding at last, although they didn't realize it yet. They would soon create an unbreakable bond for the rest of their days.

The old man continued, "You will rest here in this hovel for a day or two. Food will be brought to you by the Woman. I will let you know when it's safe to continue on your way. We have received word that some travelers have been robbed along your path close to here recently. When we feel the robbers are gone from the area and it is safe once more, you will continue on your journey. I must leave you now, as I must rest these poor old bones. You two make yourselves comfortable here. Don't worry. You will be safe here." With that the old man struggled to get up and hobbled out of the hovel.

With a worried look and a little fear in her voice, Mot told Van Ba, "I didn't know that there could be any perils by robbers in our mission. That was never spoken of to me. I was only supposed to guide you onto China. I don't how we can trust these people who are making all of these changes. How do we know where and in what manner they get all their information? And are they watching us some way while we travel? Will they lead us into some kind of a trap?"

"I expected to have a hard journey," Van Ba replied. "I didn't know I'd get a guide. No reflection on you. Like you, that part was not related to me. All of the information I had on contacts and routes have gone by the wayside. I began wondering what was going on when I was first told to disregard my documents in Binh Tuy. This raises a lot more questions for me too. We must discuss these changes and decide for ourselves what we're to do." Mot nodded to him in agreement. "As for us being watched, I have felt uneasy a few times. I thought it was just my nerves, and the physical exertion of the trip at the time, but you could be right about that. Danger that lurks cannot always be seen, it's always dark."

"I've had strange feelings also. I've spent a lot of time on trails without feeling the least bit spooky. Let us think about this and wait until after we eat to discuss it further. I'm tired and want to rest a little. Let us lay out our mats, lie down, close our eyes, and dream good dreams." With this remark, Mot began making herself a good, level, flat even spot to place her mat on the uneven dirt floor. Some hovels have rugs on the floor but this one did not. Van Ba did the same and they were soon in a light slumber.

The two began to stir a little when they heard a sound outside of the hovel. The Woman entered the hovel carrying a tray and said, "Wake up you ungrateful peons," as she sat the tray with bowls of food, same as earlier in the day, and not as hot, on the floor. "You need to eat heartily to keep up your strength for your travel. I'll be back later to retrieve the bowls." As she turned abruptly and left the hovel, the pair sat up and took their bowls and sated their hunger.

After eating their fill, Mot and Van Ba agreed that even though the Woman was a good cook, she was lacking in her personality at the very least. Not a people person for sure. She seemed to growl at them rather than speak to them. The vegetables, rice, and the bread were prepared perfectly. The only meal that could have topped it would have been having dried fish with nuoc mam sauce. They sat feeling their full stomachs for a few minutes. Then one at a time, they went out behind the hovel and relieved themselves. Now that they were feeling full and satisfied, they sat and looked at each other for a long time, waiting for one or the other to speak his/her mind. Mot looked like an angel to Van Ba when she suddenly blushed and turned her head slightly away. Van Ba, not being very sure of himself, tried being as polite as possible and asked if he could help her in any way.

"It's really nothing to speak of. I just kind of thought that you may not be the dumb, brash, and irritable man as I first thought you were. You seem to be a very strong, competent, and caring individual. It was really dumb of me to think about you that way. In my travels, I've had to put up with some real jerks I was guiding at times. I've even had to fight some off physically. That's why I studied martial arts. It seems to me it's like some men think of only one thing above all others and could care less about women's feelings."

"It was not dumb at all for you to think that way about me, and in that manner, Mot! I was way out of line the way I spoke to you" He answered her. "I have thought the same about you. I guess if you were dumb, then I was dumb too. I have never tried to take advantage of any woman, and I would fight any man I saw abusing one. I'm sorry you have had to put up with that kind of ignorance from me."

"OK, we are both dumb. You know how I see you now, so please tell me what you have thought about me. I may want to change your mind if you don't like me. I am a very good person once you get to know me."

He carped back at her, "No one would ever think you could reason like a woman, now would they?" and he laughed. Seeing the grin on his face, she thought about it for a moment or two and laughed also.

He was very adamant about his feelings regarding the mission and spoke freely about them. "I am wondering also about the trek back after getting the package. I don't think we would be bothered much on the way there. If these people he spoke of are not with the No Name, they might not know who the man is that we are to meet or what the package is, only the sub-hamlet where he'll be. They could be planning to ambush us on the way back to Nguyen Hai. Our route back may not be known to them either, so they would have to follow us. We would have to be on our guard every minute and try to evade any surveillance by an enemy, or for that matter, robbers. Since you've been in that area before, do you think that wherever this place is, you could find a different route from the one we will be given to take?"

"As much as I hate to agree with you, I do. I am very concerned for our mutual safety on the return trip. I want to live a long, healthy, and hopefully prosperous life. Maybe have some babies sometime. If we were not so committed to the No Name, I would turn you loose and return home and find a good man. I think I would worry that you made it back safely, but I will not desert you on this mission no matter what." She continued, "Finding us a different route back depends on where this sub-hamlet we're to go is. If I'm not familiar with the area, maybe we can find someone on the sly that can direct us to an area I do know well. Either way, I think we have a very serious problem ahead of us. I hope you can keep me safe."

"I'll do my best to protect you. Whether we agree or not, we are now a team, and teammates protect one another. Yes, that is a good plan about finding someone who can tell us where we need to go. I've been told where to go many times over, but that is another story." He laughed again and she smiled. "We must be very careful as to whom we ask for help though. About your other feelings, please believe in me. I pledge I will do my utmost to protect you and get you back safe and sound."

"You are so young and beautiful, and I would worry very much about your virtue and how you might be violated." She blushed again and he continued. "We must also plan how we will defend ourselves after receiving the package, if needed. Your martial arts skill will be very important to our defense. Just so you know and to set your mind further at ease, I have also had some training in the arts. That was one of the factors of my being chosen for the No Name long ago. I do have a couple of sharp knives with me too."

They talked and planned for a couple of hours in the darkness, were only interrupted when the Women retrieved the tray of bowls. Since they were farther north from where they began their journey together, the nights were a little cooler. They took raggedy blankets from their packs and lay on their mats with them and tried to sleep. After an hour, Mot felt chilled. She got up and put her blanket over Van Ba's, climbed under them and nestled her butt in to his midsection, which felt good to him. As he placed his arm over her shoulder, she sighed, snuggled down more, and they both slept a warm, wonderful, peaceful, restful sleep.

They awoke at sunrise, stretching and feeling rested for a change. Once again, each went out to the rear of the hovel to relieve themselves. It was strangely quiet in the hovel, as they were not speaking, just sitting on their haunches and looking at each other. After about an hour, the Woman came with rice, bread, and tea and placed the bowls in front of them and left without a word. They finally smiled at each other and ate their fill once more. After eating, they began to talk a little more to each other about their lives and small things in general and felt calm and relaxed with each other more than their previous days together.

While waiting, they looked at the food they had brought with them. They had to throw out the rest of their bread, as it was covered with mold. They each made a mental note of what they would need on the trail. They hoped there was a good market nearby.

Two hours later, after the Woman had already taken their bowls and cups, the old man finally arrived. He entered slowly, a little bent over and more dependent on his cane than the previous day. With a huge groan, he sat on the floor and then sighed. "I feel older than I am this morning. That's pretty old if I do say so myself," he said with a chuckle. He also noticed the two blankets lying together atop the mats. After Van Ba and Mot welcomed him back, he continued to address them.

"You two look real cheerful this morning. You even look better rested too. I've not received any news from my messenger so far today, so I'll be leaving you two alone again. I must go and await the messenger's arrival. Then I'll return here and update you. You two may do anything I'm too old to do if you want to. Ha! Ha! Oh, to be young again and in love. I remember being young and having all the pretty girls around me. It was hard for me to choose only one of them at a time." He pointed toward the mats and blankets, laughed, and then he slowly arose, awkwardly, almost falling, and left with a shuffle and a laugh.

The two travelers looked at each other and laughed too. They were sure the old man thought they had done the big nasty during the night. Mot was sure that Van Ba was probably thinking about doing it last night when she crawled in beside him and snuggled close to him to warm her body. She wondered what it would have been like with him. Although she was a virgin, many times she had tricked much older men into thinking she was not. She was used to getting a few dongs from them for her survival and then leaving them horny. Until now, Mot had never considered this as bad. She only thought of getting money to live on, as she was abandoned as a child at 11 years of age.

Surprising him, Mot asked Van Ba, "Have you had a lot of women Van Ba? Do you have a wife or girlfriend?" He looked at her with his questioning eyes.

"Why do you want to know? As I promised, I have not tried to flirt with or seduce you in any way. Is this something important to you?"

"No, I was just curious. But I would like to know more about you since we will spend a lot of time together. It would help me understand your manners and decisions better.

We must begin to think alike for our own safety. Knowing more about each other would help. I am considering telling you something about me."

"Since it's not important to you I will answer your questions. I married young and my young wife died soon after we were wed. She had been very sickly and the doctor in our hamlet didn't know what was wrong with her or how to treat her. I never desired to be married again. We were very happy what time we had together and had wonderful and meaningful sex life until she became too sick. I have always felt bad that we could not have babies before she passed. And yes, I've had a few other women over the years since then. They were nice, and I liked them, but there were none I was in love with."

"Presently there is a woman in my sub-hamlet that I like very much. She's a little older than me, middle aged, and still has a young girl's body that I like a lot, but I'm not in love with her. I call her my secret girlfriend. She really isn't my full-time woman. When we spend time together once in a while, she will cook for me and service me in many ways when I need it. I'm the only one man she'll service, even though she always feels the need too. I feel safe with her, and she with me. She is very clean in her person and in her hovel and performs for me wonderfully. She makes me feel very satisfied and alive when I'm with her, and I try my best to make her feel the same. I must say too that she is a very good cook also."

"I also work very hard most days, sometimes in the fields, sometimes in the paddies, and sometimes I go on missions for the No Name. I have sold fish, rice, and vegetables for land owners, and sometimes I help in their fields for free vegetables or in the paddies for rice. I'm not too good at farming, so I do what I can. I cook for myself too. I also have a habit of speaking my mind without thinking often, and I'm sometimes crabby. So, you can see I'm a simple, poor, humble peasant and I'm not rich. However, I am a happy, poor, humble peasant."

"I'm glad you've told me these things Van Ba. Since we met, I thought you might have been a high-ranking Mandarin in disguise, even though I hoped you weren't. I am sorry about your young wife and I hope that someday you will find the right woman and fall in love again. A man needs a good woman to cook and service him in the many ways that you men seek, and to give him many babies. I hope you will receive many riches from this journey. You've led a good life and you deserve it."

Mot continued on, telling him about her childhood, how she teased older men for money, and last, but not least, that she was still a virgin. "That is why I demanded that you not touch me. I was told when given this mission that if I were not a Virgin I should still service you as you needed. After explaining this to my contact, it was decided I would not have to do it, and that gave me relief. I'm also curious about one other thing. Have you even thought about having sex with me? You haven't seemed to accept me as a woman at all."

"Well, you know I was mad and had trouble accepting you at first because I had planned my route and was not told to expect a guide or a change of plans. I don't like surprises like that. To make matters worse, you are young, very pretty and you are built like all women should be. You also have nice eyes, kissable lips, good breasts, a nice butt, and I bet really nice legs. Exactly the kind of woman any man would want. I have looked at you and admired how you handle yourself. You are strong and terrific. To be honest with you, I have had thoughts. Last night when you laid with me and put that nice butt in my groin, I had to force myself to return to sleep to keep from getting horny. Yes, I do want you, but I will honor your virginity and I will keep my promise to you as long as you do nothing to make me even hornier for you. Oh! You look like you're blushing! That makes you even more beautiful."

"I've never had a man to be so honest and describe me like that. I am honored. Some of the things that men have said to me I will not repeat; ever. When I was abandoned as a child, a lot of men only wanted to grab at my young, developing tits and put their hands between my legs. It was hard fighting them off. That's why I trained in the martial arts. I must confess! I have used my skills against men and would not hesitate to do it again. I want to wait until I find a man that I want to have babies with before I have my first sex. Then I will give him everything he wants, whenever he wants it. This is the first time I've not been offended by a man wanting me. You are a hard man to understand, but you are honest and loyal to yourself and have a great sense of responsibility. I feel very safe and a little relaxed with you. That is something new for me as I have learned that most men cannot be trusted around a girl like me."

Before they could continue their conversation, the old man staggered into the hovel and sagged to the floor hard. "All of these trips are telling on this old man," he mumbled while wiping sweat from his face with his sleeve. "I have news. First let me catch my breath and rest these old bones." He reached over, pulled Mot's mat to him, and lay down. He was soon snoring and Van Ba and Mot were giggling at him. Neither had ever met an old man like him.

Van Ba reached over, took Mot's hand, and led her from the hovel. They walked far enough away that, should the old man awaken, he would not be able to hear them. He began, "I have had to think very hard about what I should say to you. I now know that I can trust you. You must not repeat this to any on. The mission of mine is not just to receive a package from a Chinese man, but also to gain information from him on whether or not China may be planning to invade our country once more. I hope the man with the package will have the answers for me also. My biggest worry is that someone will not want this information to be delivered."

"Oh! Oh! Shit! Shit! I did not expect this," she exclaimed. "I should have been told all about the mission, not just a little! Not told by you, but by the one who assigned me to do this work. Now I'm really scared. We must be doubly on our guard. I think maybe you're right about not being bothered on the way. If someone doesn't want the information leaked, they may wait to see if it is given to you before acting to stop you. What a mess we might be confronting."

"Those are my thoughts exactly. This is so different from going into China to receive the package and information. I bet the route we receive, I hope, will not be too high up in the mountains. This would mean an easier journey for us than going over them to China. Let us return to the hovel quietly so as not to wake the old man," he answered.

When they entered the hovel, the old man was still snoring. They sat and waited in silence. Finally, the old man snorted and jerked awake. He looked around the hovel as though he had no idea where he was at. Then his eyes focused on the pair of travelers.

To them he said, "Oh, yes. I remember now. I have some good news for you. My messenger came to me from your destination and said that the path you must follow to your destination seems to be clear. He took his time coming here; it didn't make me happy. He traveled parallel to the trails you will take and saw no trace of bandits or wonderers. There is a sub-hamlet about three days or so from here named Tra Ke #4 that you will go to. Who and what you are looking for will be located at that sub-hamlet!

"I must offer you this advice for your trek. The first thing you must always be aware of is your surroundings. You do not want to be caught off guard. Once in a while, instead of looking to your rear, kind of hide and watch your back path to see if you are followed. You must be careful when and where you build a fire to cook with or for warmth along the way, so no one will see the smoke."

"And as you have noticed, the nights are getting colder. Soon the daytime will be cold too. At night you will need to find a place where you will have some protection from the winds. I'd suggest a dense wooded area back from the trail you're on. Hopefully you will complete your trek before the really cold winds and the seasonal rains come. You must protect yourselves from the cold, and possibly rain, as much as possible. Always keep your water bladders close to your bodies, especially at night, to keep them from freezing. Water is the most important thing you need on the trail. It's hard to drink frozen water I'm told. I never tried it."

"Early in the morning before dawn, the Woman will bring you food to eat and tea to drink for your strength. She will also bring you fresh bread and vegetables for your journey. You already have rice, dried fish, and nuoc mam. After you eat, I will be here to give your route to you. When you leave here, you will see the small stream. Empty your water bladders there and refill them with fresh water. I pray for a safe journey and a successful mission for you. I must go now. Goodbye. Have a nice sleep." With that, the old man struggled to his feet and staggered out of the hovel once again."

"Oh, my Van Ba!" Mot said while seriously looking Van Ba in the eyes. "I never gave that much thought at all to the weather we may encounter along the way. I knew it was cooling at nights, but I didn't think it might be a problem. I should have realized that last night that it could when I crawled in with you for the warmth. It was very comfortable, warm, and cozy snuggled up to you with your arm around me. I really slept well." She blushed at her own words. She still couldn't understand why his arm around her during the night made her feel so safe. "I'm glad I have an extra change of clothes in my bag. I can pull them over these when I get cold. Van Ba agreed with her.

"We have some time before the Woman brings our supper, so I think I will walk to the little market in that other sub-hamlet and get two more blankets to protect us from the cold, and maybe another set of clothes. Maybe I can find a treat too. Stand up and come with me. Fresh air will make us feel good. This hovel is stuffy!" With a smile on her face, Mot grabbed their conical hats in one hand and took Van Ba's hand in the other and led him from the hovel. Van Ba couldn't believe she did this so cheerfully. It was like they had been friends forever. It was very, very strange, indeed, but it was a nice feeling to have.

Mot, being young and energetic, even had Van Ba skipping along a couple of times. He was enjoying the moment, and it pleased him to see this perky side of her. He also noticed a subtle beauty about her and her body that caused his loins to feel very stimulated. The thought of having a baby with her was teasing his mind and another body part. He almost wished this could last forever and screw the journey.

After buying blankets and more clothes and having a fruit treat at the market, they frolicked all the way back to the hovel. Mot was also having a great time. It was the first time she enjoyed being with Van Ba, not counting last night. He wasn't bad looking, he was a strong and solid man, and she bet he would be very protective of her as he had said. She couldn't help wondering what it would be like having sex and babies with him. She could do a lot worse.

"Stop thinking this way," she opined to herself. That's not what this mission is about.

Shortly after returning to the hovel, the Woman, in her seemingly constant foul mood, brought their supper. This time, however, she sat on her haunches outside the hovel until the two finished eating, then took the dishes and left in a huff.

As usual, Van Ba and Mot took turns going outside and relieving their body waste. After that ritual, Mot handed Van Ba one of the new blankets and asked him to put it on top the other two, as it was getting cooler and they would need the warmth this night. She placed the other new blanket on top of the mats. When Van Ba turned around from placing the blanket, he was shocked, his mouth gaping and looking at rare feminine beauty. Mot had pulled off her pants and was looking him in the eyes. She said, "Quit staring at me and pull your pants off. We need to get under the blankets for warmth." Van Ba shook his head from side to side in wonderment, looking at great pair of legs and where they joined, and for once he did as he was told by a woman without hesitation.

CHAPTER 4

Van Ba wasted no time obeying her suggestion. He scooted under the blankets in no time at all, and Mot crept in beside him and wiggled her firm yet soft, silky romp into his groin. "I feel so warm and safe now. Put your arm around me like you did last night. Do you like being close to me this way? I feel that you do."

Surprised by her actions, he got an erection as soon as she wiggled up to him. It really felt good. It had been a long time since a rump like hers had been pushed into his groin. She had to know how he was bothered by her body, he thought. Surely, she couldn't be that dumb. He gulped and managed a very weak, "Yes! I definitely do!" Then he managed to utter to her more strongly, "Woman, do you know what you're doing to me? I sure hope you do! You're making me hornier than any woman has ever done."

She cooed back at him, "I do know what I'm doing! I like you! I just now decided I want to have a baby with you. You don't have to marry me. Just make me happy while we're together." As she spoke, she wiggled a little more against his erection. "I told you before I would like to have children. Even to just having one baby. I don't think I will ever find a better man than you for my first." As she wiggled more, she offered, "I've never had one of those hard things against my butt before. I think I'm going to like it a lot. I can't wait until it gets to the other place." She did like it a lot!

After a couple bouts of lovemaking, they fell into a most relaxing sleep. They were awakened in the dark by the Woman carrying a lit candle and bringing breakfast and the food for their journey. She turned her back to them as they got up and got dressed. With her usual venom, she barked at the two and told them, "You two need to eat quickly, then get packed up and ready to go. I will wait inside because it's colder out there, and when you are done eating I will take the dishes and leave. The old man will be here soon. I hope I never see you two again. Your being here has been a burden on me." The Woman spoke not another word. When the two were done eating, she grabbed up the dishes, left the candle and went.

Van Ba and Mot hurriedly packed their gear, along with the fresh bread and raw vegetables and uncooked rice the Woman had brought them. Then they sat close to each other for warmth with a blanket around them. Mot reached over and took Van Ba's hand. "I have never had such a wonderful night in my life. I can't believe that the sex I've shunned for so long is so wonderful. I hope I'll have your baby. I want it because I'll never find another lover like you. I really do know that I'll never find another lover like you. You've made me feel like a real woman for the first time in my life. I only wished that you would have said sweeter things to me during the lovemaking, even though I know you don't love me."

"I was so excited I didn't know how to say much of anything. I must confess Mot. I do care for you. In fact, I think I've grown very fond of you in just a short time. It's just that I have to sort out my feelings. I've been hung up about my wife for years and never let myself feel real love and affection for any woman. I must say that I was surprised and at a loss for words because a beautiful young woman with such a wonderful body, that I like very much, made me very happy. I want you to have that baby, and I want to care for the two of you. I want to make love to you every day forever in so many ways. When our journey is complete, we must talk about marriage. I don't want to embarrass you, but you have delicious lips and a nice ass, along with great breasts, luscious thighs, and another attribute that took me to cloud nine for the first time in my life. I just can't believe how wonderful you made me feel." Just as she started to blush at Van Ba's compliments, the old man, once more, shivering from the cold, stumbled out of the darkness and cold into the hovel.

"Good morning to you my children. Whoops, I forgot, you're not my children, are you. I get people mixed up sometimes. I hope you had a good night's rest. You look like you're packed and ready to go." Not waiting for a reply, he offered, "Good! First, I want to wish you luck. Your journey is so very important, and I want it to be a successful mission. I like you two and I want you to be safe, and successful as well. I know I will be looked upon favorably by Nguyen Hai if you have success and you reach the next destination and return in one piece. You'll have the undying admiration and support from the No Name for the rest of your lives."

The old man continued to her, "Mot! Here is a crude map of your route drawn up by the messenger who came to me yesterday. It shows the trails and the very few sub-hamlets along the way. The trails will bypass some sub-hamlets in hilly areas, and they go around some hamlets and villages too. If you will take notice, sub-hamlet Tra Ke #4 is at the end of your trek. You will find whom and whatever you and Van Ba seek there." He handed the map to Mot and a folded piece of paper to Van Ba.

To him he stated, "Van Ba, I'm told you can read Chinese characters. The name of the one you must find and a proper introduction of you to him is written here in Chinese characters. Don't lose it or the mission will fail.

"A word of caution to you two. Don't forget to go by the stream for fresh water when you leave, and don't let your water bladders freeze during your journey. Wait a few minutes after I'm gone to leave here. No need for you to say goodbye. Have yourselves a safe and enjoyable journey." With that he turned and shuffled out of the hovel into the chilling, dark morning air.

As the old man left, they looked into one another's eyes and Mot said, "You said before the old man came that I had a nice ass and other things. I'm glad you like them. I'll have you know that that thing of yours is nice too, when it's hard. It's really funny looking and droopy when soft. Whatever you call it! Now that the old man's gone, let's have a good hug and kiss before we leave out of here and get on the road."

After a great hug and kiss, and a few more, they slowly picked up their gear, giving the old man more time to move away. Then they blew out the candle and put it in one of the packs and left the raggedy hovel behind them. There was no sign of the old man. Following the path in the chilling darkness, they finally came to the stream and did as the old man had recommended. They dumped out the stale water and refilled their bladders from the fresh stream, drank their fill, then refilled the bladders.

After the bladder filling, Mot said she needed another kiss before starting out again, so she took five kisses and a bigger hug than in the hovel; she even groped him a little and he responded in kind, and then they started walking. She had looked at the map carefully by candle light while still in the hovel and memorized the first three trails they would take. She hoped she could find the first one in the darkness on such a moonless night. There should be daylight out enough to find the second trail when they reached it.

Mot grabbed Van Ba's hand once again, and they both smiled at each other as they walked. It was funny for Van Ba because he had never before had a hard on while walking. This woman, he decided, was doing everything to get his goat and make him feel lost and hard up and maybe even in love. She is hot stuff for sure. He didn't lie about how her body and her sex made him feel, and he couldn't wait for the night to come. When she's hungry, he might just give her something long and round to eat. She would get her first all day sucker to work on.

Mot finally found the first path branching off to their left. It was narrower than the one they were on. She led the way. This made Van Ba a little uncomfortable. In their culture, the man's woman always walked a little behind the man, but he realized that Mot was different. She was the guide, and he knew he must live with it. Besides, she had proven that she could lead the way and read danger signs much better than he could. He looked to the east and saw a little bit of light starting to form there; soon the sun would be up and would light up their path. Feeling a little chilled from the wind and cold, he hoped that when the sun did rise it would warm them a little. He knew from experience that the nights on approaching the mountains could sometimes be really freezing.

After walking another hour, they finally came upon the second trail, just as the sun could be seen coming up over the horizon. The second trail branched off to the right and looked to be a little wider than the one they were on. Van Ba felt his legs forcing his steps and noticed that they were beginning to walk uphill. After turning onto the second trail, Mot turned to him and said, "We'll have a lot of uphill and downhill walking for some time. I think we will be on this trail until maybe tomorrow afternoon before we come to the third trail, so we need to slow down a little and conserve our energy somewhat. In a short while we'll stop and rest and have some water. Is that OK with you?"

Although huffing and puffing a bit, he answered, "As you wish my dear. Your very wish is my command, my Princes. I already feel a little thirsty, and I'm putting you on notice that I feel horny too. I'm glad the sun is rising so we can see where we're going." He stubbed his toe, tripped a little, and complained, "I hate stumbling around in the dark! It makes me feel like a clumsy water buffalo."

"Well, I thought you were a big strong and brave man, and here you are complaining already," she giggled. "Will we have to stop, fix your toe, and rest a day or two before you can continue on?"

"Go on and get moving woman and find us a good place to stop!" he responded strongly, but with a smile.

She finally found a small grove of trees that looked just right for cover, and they entered, found a clearing, put their gear down, laid down their sleeping mats, and sat on them. It felt good to be out of the chilly wind. They were both glad they had put on a second set of clothes. "It's going to be colder tonight Van Ba. We'll need to snuggle really tight for our warmth while we sleep." He heartily agreed with that and he began daydreaming about her young, lithe body.

Satisfied that they were comfortable, she took out some bread for them while he got his water bladder, took a drink, and passed it to her. After each had drunk a little water, they ate a small portion of bread. Then Mot scooted a little closer and rested her head on his shoulder. A few minutes later they had another drink, picked up their gear, returned to the trail, and resumed their pace. The sun was now in full sight and they had their daylight and a little less cold.

By noon, they had been walking for hours and were cold and beginning to tire. The trail was winding around a clump of trees, and as they were almost around it, there sat a man with his face partly hidden by his tilted conical hat. They waved to him but he didn't move. Van Ba eyed him with suspicion. When they got to him, he stood, took off his conical hat, and said to Van Ba, "I want your money and your gear and your' woman. Otherwise, I'll hurt you like you've never been hurt, then I'll have lots of fun with your woman friend for a long time!"

"Fuck your asshole with your own tongue!" Van Ba responded. At this, the man dropped his hat and leapt on him, taking him to the ground, and started to pummel him in the head. Van Ba felt helpless because of his gear's burden. Mot immediately dropped her gear and gave the man a round kick to the side of his head, knocking him unconscious. She rolled the man off of Van Ba and helped him up and then hugged him as tight as she could.

"I hope you're not hurt! I was so afraid for you. I don't ever want anything to happen to you. I hate to say so, but I know I love you!"

Rubbing his cheeks and jaw, he opined, "I'm OK Woman! I just have a couple of sore spots. Even though I had everything under my control, I do thank you for the rescue!" He laughed and in a matter-of-fact manner, stated. "May I say, Mot, that I'm feeling some love for you too, as well as a terrific desire for your most wonderful body. I never thought that after my late wife that I'd be telling another woman I love her. I really do and I want to make a lot of boy babies with you, and maybe even a girl."

The man was starting to wake, moan, and was trying to sit up, so Van Ba stepped over and kicked him in the head again, knocking him out again for good luck. The man moaned and sank back into a supine position. "We have good kicks, don't we, Mot?" She smiled at him.

Mot picked up her gear, smiled at him again, and they continued on their way, hoping there would be no more friggen bandits along the way. Farther along the trail, they were walking among large rock formations on an incline and stopped in the shelter of one to have some lunch and rest their tired bones. They ate some dried fish with nuoc mam sauce, bread, and some water. Then they sat back against the rock formation that was a little warm from the sun and took a needed short nap.

Waking up a short time later, Mot said, "I hope we can find a place like this tonight so we can make a fire, cook rice and vegetables, and drink hot tea for our warmth. We need a good meal for our strength. Do you think we should collect some wood along the way? I noticed there isn't any right around here."

"Let's wait till we see what's down the road. There must be more treed areas ahead of us. We already have heavy loads, and the breathing is a little harder this high up!" Mot agreed with him, and they continued their trek after one more drink of water.

About 300 meters later, the trail started a slight downward trend and the walking seemed slightly easier. Soon they came by a small stream flowing by the trail. They stopped to rest by it, washing their faces and hands, feeling fresher from the cool water, and refilling the water bladders. Some hugging and kissing were enjoyed, then they picked up their gear and went on down the trail. The trail had even more of a down slope to it now, and it was a great aid to their walking and breathing.

The trail had been winding down around the small mountain they were on, and as they cleared it, they could see a valley in the distance and a path leading off of it towards a far off sub-hamlet. They could see the tiny-looking farmers with their water buffalos working in their fields. As they descended, the cold and the icy wind didn't seem nearly as bad. They felt good about that and they could see a few groves of trees in the valley. These things lifted their spirits a lot. One of those groves would be a great place to cook supper, and maybe even spend the night. Van Ba was anxious to spend the night with Mot again. He hoped they wouldn't be too tired.

As they passed the trail leading to the sub-hamlet, a figure came out of the first grove. Nearing the figure, they saw it was a woman with a conical hat coming towards them. She was walking with a swinging gait and carrying two baskets suspended from a pole balanced on her shoulder. When she got closer, they saw that she was an older woman, with black betel nut teeth and darkly tanned skin. She was shriveled and skeleton-like from years of working the fields and looked much older than she really was.

The three greeted one another and talked about the weather and a few other simple things. The woman explained that she had been picking roots to cook that didn't grow near her sub-hamlet and that she needed to be home before dark or her husband would be mad. When asked, she stated she didn't know of any bandits working in the area nor had she seen any strange men about. This was a very peaceful valley with very peaceful people.

Mot asked her if there was a nice spot in this grove to cook and pass the night. The woman explained that this close one wouldn't do; however, the next grove on the left-hand side had a couple of small clearings in it that would be good for cooking and sleeping and would offer some protection from the wind as well. The woman added, "You'll be safe there too. As I said, we never have any bandits in this area, but you never know. If you are in need water, there is a stream a little way down the path from that grove." Mot thanked her very much, then they said good bye and went their separate ways.

"Wow!" stated Van Ba. "That sounds good. This load we carry is wearing us both down. Also, I'm hungry, sleepy, and tired, and I want all of you I can handle."

"Just like a man! You only have one thought in that brain in your pants," she cooed. "I'm glad of that for the first time in my life."

After the two entered one of the clearings and dropped their load, Van Ba gathered branches for a fire and Mot retrieved pots, bowls, and cups from their packs, along with the bread, rice, tea, and vegetables. Van Ba got a fire going and placed their mats on the ground close to it so they would have a little protection from the cold ground when they sat. Looking around some more, they agreed that this was a nice place to stop for the night. The two engaged in small talk while Mot prepared the food. The fire looked weak, so Van Ba got up, gathered more limbs, and put them on the fire and warmed his hands from the fire's heat. He sat on his mat and watched Mot handle her chores in a womanly manner. He's thinking, she's very competent the way she works, and she's got a great body to look at as well, especially the way her rear sways. He knew he was a lucky man. He got another erection when he saw her bend over.

Mot finished the cooking, and they moved the mats even closer to the fire to be more comfortable while they ate greedily. Van Ba really liked the food and filled his stomach to the limit. He complimented Mot with, "This is a really good meal. You should go back to that sub-hamlet and teach that Woman how to cook vegetables. This is another great reason to marry you, besides your fine body!"

"Flattering me will get you everything you want," she replied.

After eating, Mot covered the leftover rice and vegetables in the pot with a rag, and Van Ba gathered more wood for the fire, making sure there was enough for now and the next morning's fire. Then the two found their own little area of the woods to relieve themselves. When they were comfortable again, Mot suggested, "While we have a fire burning and some warmth from it, I think you should think about taking the things you need from me. I need to learn about all that we can do together. I've heard that there are many ways to please each other, and I know I want you to please me, and I want to please you very much."

Grinning he said, "As your humble and adored teacher, I have already prepared that lesson. So, student, prepare to learn!" He then began the lesson, and Mot moaned with pleasure. She was a good student and quick learner.

After making love for a while, the fire was dying and it was getting colder. He put more limbs on the fire, then they put one blanket on top of the mats because of the cold ground, got their water bladders, put the other three blankets over themselves, and curled up close together for the night. They had an exhausted but restful sleep in the comfort and warmth of each other's bodies. Even the noise made from the occasional small animals wandering the area looking for warmth couldn't wake them.

Mot awoke as the sun was coming up. She reached over and shook her teacher of the previous night and chided, "Time to get up lazy bones. You sleep and snore like a bear. We need to get a fire going again. My butt's cold."

"Woman," he answered, "I've got something that will warm your butt if you don't be still. I get the hint." He got up and rebuilt the fire while Mot prepared to make tea to drink with their bread and warmed the left-over rice and vegetables.

After they ate, they cleaned up everything, put out the fire by covering it with dirt, packed up their supplies, and went back to the trail to begin their next leg of their hike. A little way from this grove was the stream the older lady had told them about. After dropping their loads, they refilled their water bladders, washed their hands and faces even though the water was so cold, then drank their fill from the cool stream. They talked a little about their security and the lady's statement about no bandits. The bandits didn't worry them as much as someone watching them. Remembering what the old man told them, they decided that where the trail curved at the next grove they would round the curve, enter the tree line, and wait a while to see if they were being watched or followed. Once again, they packed up and started walking.

Rounding the bend, they found the right spot in the tree line and entered the wooded area. They found a nice nook close to the road to watch from and dropped their loads. Their mats were laid on the ground, and they lay on them for more comfort and protection from the cold earth. They lay in a prone position where the view of the road was clear. Soon, they observed a young man carrying a bedroll, a bag, and water bladder on the trail, slowly approaching in a seemingly cautious manner from the direction from which they came. When he was close enough, the two left their spots and stepped on to the road in front of him and looked him in the eyes. Mot said, "Good morning! Who the hell are you?"

The young man grinned at her and said, "You caught me!"

Now Van Ba spoke up, "What do you mean, we caught you. What have you been doing that you've been caught?"

"The old man sent me," he explained. "Let me put your minds to rest. The old man is superstitious, but cautious and smart. He knows how important and vital your mission is. Even though he received a report that the way was clear of bandits and suspicious people, he wanted some help for you if it was needed. I am supposed to help you if you have trouble. If the odds are too great, I'm to leave you to your fate and report back to him. The old man instructed me to tell you why I'm here if you caught me or if I had to come to your aid. I'm to follow you to Tra Ke #4 and return to him when you enter the sub-hamlet and are safe. To change the subject, you surprised me when you took out that bandit. Good kick, woman."

"Thank you," Mot replied, "but Van Ba had it under control, didn't you worthless one?" she commented while looking at her guy with a smile. "Don't forget, Van Ba got the last kick in." The young man nodded his head up and down.

Now, Van Ba reasoned, "Because you have followed us, know our destination, and have been charged with our safety and well-being, you must be from the old man. I now think he was not as old and feeble as he appeared to be. So, tell me! What is your name?"

"I am Trung Hai. I, like you, belong to the No Name. I do tasks for them when it is requested of me, the same as you two do. You are Van Ba, and the woman is Mot. You two are both well respected members. I'm glad to meet you at last. You surprised me again by catching me. I did not expect that. The old man said he had been told that you two were very good, always aware of your surroundings, and you have proved that to me. From watching you since you left the old man, I believe that whatever your mission, the right ones have been chosen to complete it."

Mot spoke quickly, "What will you do now, walk with us or follow us again?"

"No! I won't walk with you. My duty is to only observe you, and if you have trouble, to render aid if possible. I will let you move on up the trail a way and then I will follow you to Tra Ke #4 and take my leave. I'm glad you caught me. I always like to talk with such a pretty woman and a competent and able wise man. You'll feel much safer if you know I'll be there to help you. You can retrieve your loads now and be off. Have a safe journey!"

"Thank you! I hope the journey is uneventful for the three of us. Your presence makes us feel more at ease for our task. I'm sure trouble would really hinder our goals," Van Ba offered to the young man. "We are really glad you're here for us. One never knows what the future holds for any of us, regardless of our life's path."

The pair thanked the young man in advance for any aid he may have to give them, said their goodbyes, got their gear, moved on to the trail, and resumed their journey, feeling safer, but still alert. They were not sure how far Troung Hai could be trusted. They did not get good vibes from him. The old man had not said anything about having them followed. It would be much better to be safe than sorry.

What the young man didn't tell Van Ba and Mot was that if they were not able to reach the sub-hamlet, Tra Ke #4, he was to continue their mission. He also neglected to tell them about another part of his own mission. He would not leave anyone alive in Tra Ke #4 to talk about the mission, and he would secure the Jade Cross for himself.

The lovers also didn't know that if they made it to the sub-hamlet, and found what they were sent for, there would be another watcher to follow and protect them all the way to their next destination. That man left the day before Van Ba and Mot so they wouldn't meet him on the trail. Trung Hai had no idea what they might be told or directed to do at Tra Ke #4 after getting that icon. He wasn't even curious about it because they would not be able to complete the mission as they would no longer exist. If the No Name wanted him to know what was to be done with the prize, they would have told him. After giving the two a head-start, he picked up his gear and continued on his own personal mission.

After passing the last wooded area and traveling about two miles, they were surprised to see the third trail cut off to the right so soon. They thought it would be much later in the day when they would reach it. Starting down it, they could see what looked to be foothills a short distance ahead. They sighed as they looked at them and continued alertly on their way, Mot in the lead as usual. The chilling wind had picked up when they started up the first foothill, and they felt it on their hands and face, so they lowered their heads, tied down their conical hats, turned into the wind blowing in to them, then plodded on up the trail. This climb would be a real test for their endurance and perseverance. Each step became a monumental task, sapping at their strength and causing aching in their backs and legs. However, they plodded on as best they could, one foot in front of the other.

CHAPTER 5

FIGHTING THE COLD AND the icy wind the duo, Van Ba and Mot, struggled up the steep trail. Their breathing became panting, harder, and their loads got heavier, and several times they felt like calling it quits. When they got those feelings, they would stop and give support and comfort to each other and to do their best to encourage each other's endurance. Their endurance was nearly sapped when the trail began its downward slope. Mot stopped them at that point. They took off their loads, laid down their mats and lay on them to rest. They pulled two blankets over themselves, cuddled together for warmth and to have a little protection from the wind. While hugging him tighter Mot whispered into Van Ba's ear saying, "I hope this fucking wind changes direction some on the way down. I know we are both exhausted. After a short rest we will make it down this trail and up and over the next foot hill."

Van Ba liked her positive attitude. He really had quite a woman on his hands. He was so happy to have found someone like her to love. He'd never met any other Vietnamese Woman with her strength and perseverance, the way she plodded on, putting one foot in front of the other. Not only that, but being young, beautiful and a having wonderful body like hers made him the luckiest man ever, in Vietnam or the world for that matter. Thinking of her this way he felt a little aroused, but this was not the time or place. They kissed, hugged tighter and then both fell into an exhausted and fitful sleep.

When they awoke an hour and a half later on, they ate some bread and dried fish with nuoc mam sauce and slaked their thirst. Their water was iced cold and very refreshing. Mai took out the map drawing the old man had given her and tried to figure out where they were and how much farther they had to go. She showed Van Ba the map drawing and pointed to where she believed they were and commented.

"Van Ba, it looks like when we get to the top of the next foot hill there will be a long decent on a winding trail that eventually straightens out and no more going up-hill before we reach Tra Ke #4. Once we start down it we'll have maybe a day and a half to reach the sub hamlet. I'll be so glad to get there. I know you will be too. I hope we can find a place for shelter and something for a fire to cook on and for spending the night on that foot hill. We really need the rest. I think I need something else too if you think you'll be able to. Will my little guy be too tired to stand up for me?" she uttered as she groped him with a smile on her lips?

"I think we can find a place and make a nice warm fire and get some of that thing you've begun to like? Don't say anything Woman. I want the something you got as well. I just hope we have enough energy left to do it fifteen times or more."

"Huh!" was Mot's reply as she gave him a light slap between his legs.

Bending over and pretending to groan from the slap Van Ba leaned over and kissed her tenderly and suggested they relieve themselves, packed up and got ready to go their way. Mot agreed.

Just then, from out of nowhere, two raggedy looking ruffians approached them. Their hair was long and scraggly, they had only partial facial hair, some rotten and some missing teeth were making them look ugly as a dog. Their clothes, what was left of them were tattered and torn; their body odors left something to be desired. The larger, and the ugliest one ordered the pair to, "Leave all your gear and what Dong you have on the ground there and run for your lives before we decide to kill you. On second thought, you, pointing at van Ba leave quickly, the young lady stays with us."

Van Ba replied, "Hey! Asshole are you serious? You may want to think about this twice. You have no idea who or what we are. It's you that needs to leave before you piss me off."

The two guys started toward Van Ba but pulled up short when suddenly Van Ba pulled his long knife and pointed it at them. Since they were unarmed they took off running down the trail in the direction from which Van Ba and Mot had come from.

Mot blinked her eyes at Van Ba and uttered, "MY hero! You saved my honor! How will I ever be able to pay you?"

He commented to her, "Hush woman, let's hit the road."

Since they had left the young man who claimed he was their observer and protector the two kept a sharp eye out for him. Even though they had seen neither hide nor hair of him his presence was felt. As they had talked between each other along the way trusting the man completely was not in their best interests. Approaching near the top of the last foothill a little nook was found. They stopped to take a break and hid there for a while to see if the young man could be seen following them. When there was no sighting of him after a while they continued on to the top and began their decent to the low lands. Mot's wish came true. As they descended the foot hill the wind was not as strong and had a slight change of direction. Both Van Ba and Mot breathed a sigh of relief being close to the bottom that they were nearly through with the foot hills. Down the winding trail a way they could see a wooded area and decided to make camp there for the night.

Reaching the wooded area, they found a little clearing among the trees big enough for a safe fire and camping. Van Ba told Mot, "You gather some fire wood and I'm going to circle around to the trail and watch for our supposed friend. I shan't stay there very long. I'll be back in no time to start the fire." He gave her a light kiss on the cheek and was gone. When he returned Mot had some twigs and branches laid for his fire and was getting out her cooking utensils and food. He got the fire going and they sat on their mats enjoying the warmth and waiting for it to become just right for cooking. After cooking, eating, what was now a usual night of pleasure and sleep, they arose, had breakfast of leftovers, and began the last lap of this segment of their journey. They did wait and watch the trail for a few minutes before stepping from the tree line to continue on.

Traveling downhill was wonderful. It had lifted their spirits and the banter between them. Mot caused an elated cry from Van Ba when almost to the straightway of the trail she looked him in the eyes and chirped, "I hope soon I'll know if I carry your son." She thought he was going to faint dead away after his joyous cry. "Men," she retorted. Her face was beaming and her smile was as big as the world had ever seen on a woman.

Reaching the straight part of the trail the wind was nearly none existent and it seemed a little warmer outside. The countryside was very unique and picturesque. This made their walking much more pleasant and less tiresome. Though still cold and a little achy, at times they would hop, skip and laugh at nothing at all together. Neither one had ever been so happy, even knowing there could still be some perils ahead. This was the most they had been motivated to walk in a few days. Van Ba's head was in the clouds just thinking of maybe being a father and what it would feel like. Would he be a stern one? Maybe he would be a laid back one? He would be a loving, caring Father at all times, that he knew for sure. Time would tell.

Late in the day back in a wooded area along the trail they could see an abandoned sub-hamlet with five or six-run down hovels. They walked through the trees to the ruined hovels and noticed a dried-up stream bed nearby. That was probably why the sub hamlet had been abandoned. Some of the roofs and sides were caved in or had holes in them, and they looked carefully through each one. The one with the most roof left and sides intact was selected to spend the night in. They were elated they had found some partial shelter. It had been a few days since they had enjoyed a roof over their head at night. They could have a small fire and it would be much warmer and comfortable at night and maybe they could have more and better sex.

The first task was getting a small branch with lots of leaves on it to sweep the accumulated debris from inside the structure. After sweeping the hovel a small fire was built under a large hole in the roof where it wouldn't burn down the place. They rested a while then took care of their usual nightly chores of cooking, eating, love making, reliving themselves, and had the best restful sleep since leaving the old man's hovel a couple of days before.

They awoke refreshed and ready to complete their journey. They ate, put out the fire, packed up and started down the trail. Their spirits were really high knowing they would be in Tra Ke #4 before the day was over. Hopefully they would be arriving sooner than dusk. Once they arrived, at their destination, they would start the next phase of their mission. Find out where the Chinaman is, and receive the intended package he has for them and deliver it to Nguyen Hai.

The only thing they needed now though was to find a clear stream to refill their water bladders. Each one only had a few small sips left. Periodically they would pause and look behind to see if there was any sign of being followed. Two hours later they came across a stream just off the dusty trail. They filled their bladders, washed hands and faces in the icy water, drank lots of water, snacked, then they continued on, enjoying the walk as much as their burden would allow.

When the sun was just past its peak in the sky, they could see men working their fields and what appeared to be a large sub-hamlet far ahead. Both jumped for joy. It had to be their destination, Tra Ke #4. They stopped and hugged and kissed for a few minutes. It was decided that they would now walk at a slower pace since the end of this journey was at hand and they didn't want to be too tired upon entering Tra Ke #4 and begin seeking the Chinaman.

As they were almost into the sub-hamlet, they could see that it was spread out and looked as if there could be about twenty or more hovels there. It was larger than they expected it to be. The huts were well spread apart. There were kids running around, women standing with their babies on hips talking to each other, some wearing conical hats, some bare headed, some cooking outside and some shopping in a little market place in the center of the complex.

They could see a few women beating the dry grown rice, the Vietnamese staple food. It was theorized that two methods of cultivating rice, one was dry in dry fields in upland areas and one wet in areas near rivers, deltas and paddies diked for water collection in waist high ponds, was developed during the Neolithic Area by groups of extended families in small communities and had not changed.

There were no men in sight as they were all out working in the fields. The women and kids looked at them with caution and the women talked fast to each other in their high-pitched tonal language. As they passed by and heard some words of fear and concern, Mot commented, "They don't know what to think of us. They probably don't see many travelers or strangers here and think the worst of us." Van Ba nodded in agreement. She was so right as always.

The duo walked into the market place, which was only on one side of a lane because it was small market, looked at the various vegetables, breads, dried fish and assorted wares. They nodded and said hello to the venders as they passed them. They asked a few of them if they had seen a Chinaman around and didn't get any real answer. However, Mot found out from one of the old women venders that there were a couple of empty hovels at the far end of the sub hamlet and they could stay there a couple of nights if they cared to. It seemed the hovels had belonged to elderly people who had passed away and the huts had not been claimed. For lack of a better plan, they left the market place and found one of the two empty hovels and made themselves at home. They felt lucky because this one had a fire pit outside for cooking and a small table with three chairs inside. Mot cleaned dust off the table and chairs as best she could and they sat on chairs at a table for the first time in many days.

"It looks like we may have a big problem finding the Chinaman we seek. Since the Chinaman is not known to the vendors in the market-place I think he must be using a Vietnamese name, if he is even here." Van Ba lamented, "I hope we haven't come this far for nothing. That would be the shits."

"It'll be all right my man. Have faith in Buda! We'll find him one way or another and be on our way in no time. He may even find us first. That would be great."

Both were tired so they napped awhile. When they awoke it was time to build a fire in the outside pit and for Mot to perform her magic with the food. It was nice eating at the table with Mot in this hovel. It made Van Ba feel that this is what the rest of their lives would be like after this mission and he liked it, he was sure she liked it too. The third chair is where the baby would sit when it grew some. While eating they decided to throw out some of their old food stuffs and get some fresh from the market before leaving Tra Ke #4. Their bread was cold, hard and would soon become moldy

After eating and still sipping tea they were surprised and shocked by a middle-aged man, slim, with a drooping mustache, weathered, and who looked a little Chinese come into the hovel. He waved a friendly hand at them and put on a crisp smile. "Hello! I'm very sorry to have startled you. I heard gossip going throughout the sub hamlet women that two travelers, a man and a woman, arrived today tired and needing a hovel to rest in. I thought I'd check to see if you needed anything and if so, how can I help you? I see you've made yourselves comfortable. It seems you have all you need. That's great. If you need to bathe or need water for cooking there is a waist deep stream just a short way behind this hovel. It's the best water in the area."

"Yes! You did startle us a lot. You could have called to us from the entrance. It's not polite to just walk in on people. So, tell me, sir, why on earth do you desire to come here and offer to help strangers like us? It seems really odd." replied Van Ba. "We, my sister and I, are merely two poor ragged and tired nomads wondering to no place in particular, trying to find a decent life for ourselves some place, so far we've had no luck at all." He put his hand inside his tunic and grasped his knife handle just in case this guy was trouble. We were told by an old woman on the trail that we might find work here.

The man, wary about Van Ba's hand in his tunic, continued, "I have heard that a couple of important travelers may stop here to visit an esteemed Chinese elder and if so, they should be treated with the utmost dignity and respect."

"Do you think that we are the ones you are expecting?" Mot, taking the lead again, commented further, "We very well could be bandits or even worse, killers. You could be in deep trouble with us. We have nothing to lose by robbing and killing for what we need. And sometimes we even like it."

"Possibly that is so. It's a position I must risk at all costs. Let me ask you your names and I will know if you are the ones."

Van Ba said, "What if we have No Name. How would you know who we are and what would you do if we are the ones?"

Picking up on the words, No Name, the man continued, "Troung Van Ba and Tran Thi Mot of the No Name are the ones I'm looking for. When I find them, they will have a proper paper of introduction. I'm sure you two tired, sad and ragged looking individuals could never be them in a million years. I'm told he is handsome devil and she is very beautiful. That description doesn't fit either one of you."

Ignoring the man's comments with restraint and releasing the knife handle Van Ba took the letter of introduction from his tunic and handed it to the man. "I think this is what you want to see if you read Chinese. If you can't, please return it to me and be on your way or get your comeuppance by my knife!"

Scanning the letter and nodding his head up and down the man said, "This is the letter of introduction to Mr. Hu that I need. We didn't expect you for another day. You have made good time traveling to here. First, I am not Mr. Hu. My name is not very important so I'll not give it to you. However, I am a member of the No Name and work with and take care of Mr. Hu. I will take you to meet him in the morning after you've had breakfast. Second, He feels you need a good night's rest after your long and tiring trek, be well fed and in good spirits when you meet. He has much information and a package for you. He is entertaining an elderly local lady tonight or he would have come to you himself. As old as he is, he does very well with the ladies."

Continuing the man begged them to forgive the bad comments about them. "I needed to be sure you are the ones we've awaited. Imposters and liars cannot be tolerated. I was satisfied when I saw the disgust on your faces from my insult. I compliment you on your calmness and self-control. Van Ba you are a handsome devil and Mot, you are as beautiful as I was told. I bet Hai Ba Chi Em (the Trung Sisters, Trung Trac and Trung Nhi), who led an uprising against us Chinese for three years, 39 AD–42 AD, could not have been more so. I'm very pleased to meet you two."

They thanked him for the compliments and indicated it was great to meet him also. After a little more conversation, the man left and the pair tidied up and prepared for the night. There was some straw in a corner of the hovel and they spread it out and put their mats on it. They then went out to the stream, took off their clothes, rinsed their bodies and fondled each other while doing so and filled their water bladders. The water and the cold soon chilled them to the bone and they dressed and hurried back to the hovel for warmth and comfort.

When they finally lay together for the night Van Ba asked if she was hungry. She wondered what he had in mind and said so. He giggled and informed her, "I was thinking of giving you something long and round to eat on." She answered, "Oh, what!" And then he fed her. Afterwards she fed him. It turned into a great night.

As promised the middle-aged man came for them after they were done eating a small breakfast and had cleaned up. He led them around several hovels and bade them enter a large one. Inside there sit an elderly man sitting on a mat with his legs crossed yoga style. He was a little chubby with white hair, a long beard and was dressed like a Mandarin. For his age he looked very good. He was smiling at them and indicated for them to join him on the large decorative mat. After they were seated the elderly man greeted them. The duo greeted the man with the proper respect due to elders.

"I am Mr. Hu, the man you're here to meet, and I'm a Master Carver from China. I was told that you were looking for me in the market place. The vendors here do not know we are Chinese so they were of little help to you. We've been staying here for a few months and we use Vietnamese names and we look very much like them. It is very important that they do not know who we are or why we are here. Please sit, relax and be comfortable. You have had a long hard journey and you should enjoy your success up to this point as long as possible. A lady friend will be here shortly to serve us hot tea. My man has gone to fetch her and the tea. Until then, you must have many questions and I will answer what I can as honestly as I can."

Mot knew she must not speak now so she sat silently as was the way of the Vietnamese women's lives. She just sat, watched, and listened to Van Ba with a sense of pride. His first comments were to offer his respect for Mr. Hu and how elated he was to be his humble servant. Then he stated, "I've been told so little about this mission I'm on and the changes that were made after beginning it I do not know what questions to ask. So, I wait to be enlightened by you as to my duties to you, my honorable master. I'm here to serve your every desire."

"Please, Nguyen Van Ba. Do not call me Master unless it pertains to carving precious jewelry, I am a Master Carver only. I carve with precious stones and gems. We both serve the No Name equally so you are not a servant to me nor am I to you. I know that you were informed of receiving a valuable package and a document for Nguyen Hai from me. I'm sure you are curious about them. It sounds like our tea is arriving now. We will continue after we drink."

Mr. Hu's aid came in with a middle-aged lady and a tray of cups, bread on a plate and a large pot of hot tea. Mot had expected an elderly woman and was surprised that the woman was middle aged and still pretty, had her hair pulled back and she seemed to be only half of Mr. Hu's age. Mot thought he was a lucky man. She also noticed Van Ba smiling at the women. She felt a tinge of jealousy and then she dismissed it. She knew her man. The tea was delicious as well as hot and the fresh bread made them feel good inside. The woman and the aide sat at the edge of the mat until the tea and bread were gone then took the tray and dishes and left the hovel to the three.

Mr. Hu began anew. "Now I will tell you why you are here. I have masterly carved a cross from a large and rare piece of jade and inlaid jewels on it. It took nearly a year and a half to carve, polish and insert the precious gems in it. I finished it four months ago. I will tell you the history of it and why."

"You are both familiar, I presume, with Tran Hung Dao the famous Vietnamese General who routed my people, as some of my ancestors were Mongol. It seems he had kept a few high- ranking Chinese prisoners just to gather information. One of them knew that as soon as the General was finished with him, he would be slaughtered or beheaded. He asked one of his keepers to take him to the General. He informed the General that if the General would release him he could get him a very large piece of rare jade from its hiding place. The General agreed to spare him and sent three warriors with the prisoner to retrieve the jade from its hiding place. When the jade was found the warriors followed orders, killed the prisoner and brought his head and the jade, maybe the largest piece of it ever to be found, to the General."

It is told that after the General wrote his masterful works on booby traps and guerrilla warfare and when he passed away the jade disappeared. It was found during the Le Loi regime and disappeared again. Someone in the family of our leader, Nguyen Hai found the jade about twenty years ago. Three years ago, he found me, due to my reputation of being a radical master carver in China, and asked me to carve the jade into a cross with inlaid jewels for the No Name. It is to be the cult's icon. After long discussions with him I agreed to become a member of the No Name and to carve the cross for him. I also agreed to use my resources to find out what China's intentions are towards Vietnam."

"When I was finished with the carving, and the inlays, I notified Nguyen Hai by messenger. You were selected to make a secret journey to China to retrieve and deliver the Jade Cross to Nguyen Hai. I could not trust it with the messenger. In the meantime, it was sadly learned that the information on your trip was compromised somehow so we changed the delivery point to here, but let it be known the old plan was still in effect. You weren't told that it would be changed on the way in order to fool the enemy. The suspected leak died the death of a thousand cuts. We changed plans and inserted a female guide to make you look like innocent travelers. We also set up watchers to protect you two along the way. One followed you here and a different one will follow you when you leave. It will be a different route from which you came here. My wish is that there will be no problems for you on your way back to Nguyen Hai."

"Van Ba, When my man returns, I will have him get the Jade Cross from where I hid it and I will give it to you. I think that you both will be amazed when you see that Jade cross. It is eighteen inches tall; the cross bar is eleven inches across and it's about an inch thick. You will need to protect it not only in your bag from damage, but with your life against bandits, assassins or No Name enemies. It must get to Nguyen Hai and the No Name no matter the cost. I hope you will not have to forfeit your wellbeing or your lives pursuing your charged duty." Very perceptive, Mr. Hu saw a slight look of fear in Mot's eyes and a twist of her lips. Van Ba didn't look much different either.

Mr. Hu's aide returned and Mr. Hu sent him to retrieve the Jade Cross. They had buried it along the trail for its safety before they entered Tra Ke #4 even though it would be lost forever if something happened to them. At least the No Name's enemies wouldn't have it.

Van Ba and Mot were still quiet and listening and Mr. Hu went on. "There is also a letter I received a couple of weeks ago from a high ranking Chinese Official, who I will not name, that describes China's present intentions towards Vietnam that you will get along with the Jade Cross. It is also very important that it be delivered too. I think Nguyen Hai will be very, very, happy not only with the icon, but with the contents of the letter. It is sealed for it is his eyes only. I know what it says, but I cannot tell you what. It is now for Nguyen Hai's eyes only."

When Mr. Hu was finished with his narration, he looked at Van Ba and asked if he had any questions now.

Van Ba queried, "Do you think there will be trouble on the return trip? I'm not worried for myself as much as I am for Mot. She might be carrying my child. I don't want any harm to come to them. It would be the end of my world if they were harmed."

"I cannot honestly guarantee your safety. We have done everything possible to keep this secret and to keep you from harms-way. Alas, I cannot predict for you what is out of my hands."

Mr. Hu looked at Mot. "You have been very quiet and patient my dear. I was told that you never hesitate to state your thoughts. I can see the gears turning in your beautiful head so tell me what's on your mind."

"Well Sir! I'm worried about my carrying Van Ba's baby and for its and his safety. I've come to love him very dearly. I was not afraid when we fought off bandits on the trail, however for some reason I suddenly feel afraid for us. I do not want us to fail in our mission nor do I want any harm done to us. I feel mixed up!"

As Mr. Hu was saying, "I understand you my child and my fears are with you," the aide returned with the Jade Cross and a sealed letter. The cross was wrapped in three rags for protection and looked bigger than Van Ba and Mot expected.

CHAPTER 6

Mr. Hu laid the Jade Cross on his lap and very carefully unwrapped it. Van Ba and Mot, as well as the aide who had not seen it unwrapped since it had been completed, were wide-eyed and stunned. It was absolutely the most beautiful icon they had ever seen. It was a real masterpiece. It would definitely be an icon for any movement. They knew Nguyen Hai will be so pleased to receive it and to use it to its maximum.

Mr. Hu told them, "It took me over a year to create this. It had to be done in complete secrecy. I had to call in many favors to obtain the various precious stones without being arrested by the rulers; plus the jade was very hard to cut and polish by hand. Very time consuming. It is the ultimate masterpiece for me though. I could never create anything to compare to this, ever again. When it's time for me to go, I will know I have done my best, and I will proudly pass on to meet my ancestors very satisfied of my creation and with the hope that the people will concur. This Icon will be the Icon of uniting all of our people."

Mr. Hu let each one hold and admire the Jade Cross. They tested its heft, ran their hands over it, oohed and aahed not only over how smooth and shiny it was, but also at how awesome the hue of the jade was. it was just like a baby's butt, they thought. Not one of the three could imagine the labor and the love Mr. Hu had put into the masterpiece. It was just unbelievable. All the different jewels sparkled, but the large red ruby inset at the intersection of the upright and crossbar was magnificent. Its blood red and seemed to radiate a glow without any light touching it. The aura it cast seemed unnatural. After it was admired by all, Mr. Hu carefully rewrapped it up again and handed it to Van Ba.

"Take this icon into your custody and protect it with your life Van Ba. Deliver it to Nguyen Hai with my blessings, and with timeliness and propriety. Then, and only then can you be proud that you were the one chosen to receive it and that you performed your duties with due diligence and honor that only a Viet could do. You must keep the pride of your successful mission as long as you have breath to take." Looking at Mot, he told her, "That goes for you also my dear. You have been an important part of Van Ba's journey and will continue to be until the end of your known world."

Mr. Hu then handed Van Ba a two-page letter sealed with wax. "This contains two pages. The first page has the directions you must follow to find Nguyen Hai. The second page inserted is sealed separately. It has very important information for Nguyen Hai's eyes only. I do not know the wording of it, but I feel it is good news about China's present posture towards the future of your country.

"Do not open the directions until you get to a certain place. You will continue on the trail that brought you here, heading east. You will travel a short distance and come to a road turning to your right, going south. Follow that turn till you come to another right turn, and walk a small way till you find a run-down and abandoned pagoda. Then, and only then, may you stop and open the directions. You must follow the path it directs you to, and I fervently hope, it will be a safe route to your success. Be always vigilant in your journey home and make sure you are not being watched along the way. There are those who would kill you, torture you, and rape your woman for this icon. Do you or your woman have any questions relating to anything before I dismiss you to do your duty to the No Name?"

Van Ba put the papers inside the makeshift pocket of his tunic. "Yes! I must ask again. We caught a man on the route here who said his duty was to follow us and offer us his protection if it was needed. He told us that there will be someone else to watch over us on this leg of our journey. Is this really true?"

"Yes, you will have a watcher, but you will not see him. He will be invisible to you. He was chosen to watch over you on this leg of your journey because of his talents and dependability. He is called the Invisible One. He is a superb fighter, has been successful at many missions for the No Name, can be trusted completely, and is deeply dedicated to Nguyen Hai and to the No Name. I hope you will be safe enough with him in the background. If anything happens to you two, he has orders to recover the cross and complete your mission."

Van Ba thanked him, then looked at Mot and asked her if she had any further inquiries of Mr. Hu. She responded, "No. I've no questions for him. I'm just ready to get this started and to get over with as soon as possible."

Then he turned back to Mr. Hu and said, "I've no further questions either Mr. Hu. I find I must compliment you on your expertise in designing and crafting the Jade Cross for Nguyen Hai and offer his thanks and admiration of your work on it and for the secret information on China. I also want to offer our thanks to you for planning the last half of our journey for us." Mot smiled at Mr. Hu, who nodded, and she nodded back in agreement. "We have been concerned about not knowing what way we would go."

"Off with you two love-birds then," Mr. Hu ordered with a big grin, "and get a good night's sleep and an early start. It's a long, hard trip ahead of you. Don't forget to go to the market and replenish your food." The four bowed to each other, and the travelers left for the hovel they were staying in.

When they got inside their hovel, they carefully placed the Jade Cross in Van Ba's bag. Looking at his loved one, Van Ba suddenly exclaimed, "Damn it! I forgot to ask Mr. Hu a very important question. I will go back there and find out a piece of information we may need along the route. I'll only be gone only a few minutes."

"I'll stay here, but I'll miss you the whole time you're gone," she kidded. If you find a pretty woman on your way there tell her I said 'Hi,' and you two have fun in the sun. She kissed him on the cheek and he was gone.

Van Ba left the lover's hovel and took his time walking to Mr. Hu's. It was a nice day out, even though there was a strong chill in the air, and the clouds were sparse but beautiful in the light blue sky. He really loved this kind of day. If it was a little warmer it really would be very nice. Hopefully it would be nice like this when they left the next morning. He wanted to ask Mr. Hu what would happen to Mot if they were accosted along the way and he was killed and she lay there injured. Would the Invisible One help her? He needed to know that if Mot was hurt, and especially if she was pregnant, she would be cared for the rest of her life. Mr. Hu may not know the answer, but Van Ba would ask anyway.

As he approached Mr. Hu's hovel, he heard moans, groans, and sounds of a scuffle. He knew immediately that something was wrong. As he ran toward the hovel he slipped one of his knives from his tunic, held it down along his leg, and quietly entered the hovel. When he got inside, he saw Trung Hai bending over the hacked and bloodied bodies of Mr. Hu and his aide with a bloody knife in his right hand and a malevolent look in his eyes.

The man looked up at him. "So we meet again, Van Ba. You're wondering what I'm doing killing these two. It's really simple. I'm going to deliver the item you have to Nguyen Hai. He'll believe me when I tell him that every one of you was killed by bandits or enemies, except your woman. I, of course, saved her in a heroic manner. She'll belong to me now and will not dare to correct me in front of Nguyen Hai. I'll have all the glory and riches, not to mention a lot of good sex with her. She's quite a sexy woman. The glory I receive will be for my fearless execution of the duty that would have been yours. And I know the sex will be the best I've ever had. I've masturbated while I watched you two do it several times. She is something. I know you two didn't know I was watching you, and that excited me too. So now it's my time with your Mot. Troung Van Ba, get ready to meet my knife and your ancestors."

With that announcement, he lunged at Van Ba, thrusting his knife straight at his heart. Van Ba sidestepped a quarter turn to his right, and as the knife narrowly missed his body, he wrapped his left arm around Trung Hai's right elbow, lifted up on it, and slashed his own knife up and across the throat of the man. Trung Hai's eyes got big, a gurgling sound came from his throat, and as his blood spurted in a stream from his carotid artery, he slumped to his knees, his eyes staring at Van Ba in disbelief. Van Ba let him fall to the ground and die. Trung Hai would never know that Van Ba was very competent in the martial arts also and had felled many foes during his adventures. He checked the other two bodies. They were definitely dead. Van Ba felt very emotional over their loss to the world because of an unworthy ass. Nguyen Hai would not be happy over this turn of these events.

Van Ba cleaned his knife on the turd's tunic, searched the hovel and found clothes that must have been the aide's and exchanged them for his outer bloodied ones. He found nothing of value in the hovel or Trung Hai's gear that he needed to take with him, so he walked slowly back to Mot so as not to draw attention.

He knew he was lucky because the hovels in this part of the sub-hamlet were not close together, and this one was at an extreme edge, so the ruckus might not have been heard. It could be only a short while before the bodies stank enough for someone to check on the hovel though. He and Mot needed to get their gear packed up and get out of the area as soon as possible. There would be no time for them to visit the marketplace here. They would have to do with what food they had until they found another marketplace.

Entering their borrowed hovel, Van Ba ordered Mot, "Pack up your gear woman! We need to slip out of here now. Quickly! Don't ask me any questions. I'll fill you in when we're on the trail." They hurriedly got their gear repacked, left the hovel walking slowly, hand in hand to avoid suspicion. They were very thankful that it was near the edge of the sub–hamlet, and where it circled around to the main trail.

Once they were clear of the sub-hamlet and walking at a quick pace, Van Ba told Mot what had happened in Mr. Hu's hovel and what he was forced to do to Trung Hai. She understood as he cursed the murderer every way he knew how to. They soon came to the first right turn and followed it. "It will be strenuous on us, but we must put as much distance between us and Tra Ke #4 as quickly as possible. We don't need any enraged people finding us. We'll surely be blamed for it if the bodies are found too soon. If it's within a day or so, we may not be suspected. I certainly hope it's the latter."

Quickening the pace even more, Mot answered, "We'll be all right my love. You'll see. Our only worry about it being found out today would be Mr. Hu's woman friend. Let's hope she's not horny and planning to be with Mr. Hu any time today. Look up ahead, Van Ba. It's our next right turn already."

They took the right turn and walked a short distance and stopped. Off in the near distance was a rundown pagoda. The walls were crumbling, and it looked like the roof had caved in some time ago. They were in the right spot. They moved back off the road to the Pagoda, put down their' gear, and Van Ba took the letters from his tunic, unsealed the outer one, then put the other one back in his pocket; still sealed. The letter was written in Chinese characters just as his letter of introduction to Mr. Hu had been. This one looked to be written by a different person and had beautifully drawn characters.

He read the letter to Mot. It said the original route to be taken had been compromised, and the second right turn took them away from that route. They were to continue up this trail, and the Invisible One would find them farther on and give them the new directions.

Looking perplexed, Mot inquired of Van Ba, "I'm really confused now. We were getting fresh food, and we were not supposed to leave Tra Ke #4 until tomorrow morning, so how will we eat and how will this man find us?"

"I'm sure he will eventually find us if he is as good as Mr. Hu said he was. I've heard of him several times at Nguyen Hai's. Never got to meet him though. It's possible that the man may have been watching and saw us leave. Right now, our best bet is to keep going at a quick pace for a time. Before we take a rest, we must be as far from Tra Ke #4 as we're able. If the bodies are found, the people may search for us. We need to find a place where we can hide and

70

watch the trail while we rest. I sense that we're in danger. We must be careful, my dear. My senses never fail me when they sense danger."

"Since you're a man and, a very experienced one at that, experienced in situations like this, I know your wisdom will get us through this trip safely. I believe in you Van Ba, and I know you'll do your best to keep us safe! I don't have your experiences in handling or fighting in dangerous situations, but I'll be beside you no matter what happens. You're stuck with me now and forever. If we don't live through this, I want you to know I have learned to love you very much."

"I fallen deeply in love with you too, woman. We'll win! You'll see! We will live and we'll raise that baby together. You'll see. Now, hush up and let's get going. We need to put some more distance between us and that sub-hamlet." They moved on up the trail with Mot in the lead as usual, moving at a very quick pace that would soon tire them even more.

Mot knew that when Van Ba called her woman, it was with respect. Many men meant the term derogatorily as an insult to their women. Van Ba was very different from other men. He was a proud man, had a strong constitution, and was honest in his feelings and dealings with her. She could never, ever put her faith in any man other than him. He was a rock, and lucky her, he was her rock.

Another two hours of a fatiguing pace went by before they found a wooded area a couple of hundred yards off the trail, and they were pleased at the clearing they found in it. Their feet and legs were hurting, their bodies ached, and they were exhausted from the fast pace and heavy loads. They were careful entering into the tree line, covering their steps behind them so as not to leave a sign that someone had entered there. When they found a good spot, they lay on their mats with a blanket over them and watched the road. Soon both of them nodded off. When they woke up, they devoured some of the hard, stale, and nearly moldy bread they had, along with the old water from their water bladders. It was a very welcome, but unsatisfying meal.

Still feeling tired and achy after they ate, they decided to stay a little longer in this comfortable spot. After discussing the situation, they decided they may even travel some at night. They could eat dried fish and nuoc mam for supper and would not need a fire. The weather was still cool, though not as cold as it was in the foot hills. The pair knew they could now slow the pace and walk in a less tiring manner, but they decided not to go too slowly. After a while, they got back on the trail. Their spirit was not as high as it had been. The killings had amplified their fears and gave them a sense that peril may lie ahead of them. They continued on in silence at a moderate pace, and once more they felt their legs and loads getting heavier with each step.

After a while, Van Ba sighed, "Mot, we must rethink about tonight. We are wearing ourselves down. The fast pace we started with took a lot out of us. It's getting close to sundown. Over there, about forty or fifty meters to the south, is a wooded area. I think we should carefully go there now and stay for the night. We can't have a fire for warmth and cooking, but I think we will fare well even so. What do you think, Mot?"

"I agree. I've never been so exhausted on the trail before this. The times I guided was slow and easy going, not stressful at all. With our being over there, we can watch the trail easier without anyone seeing us. With our mats, blankets, and body warmth all cuddled up, I think we will be OK." She stuttered a little, and he asked her what was wrong. "I wondered if we would be able to have sex tonight. For some reason or other, I feel horny. What about you and that hard thing of yours that you use for brains?"

"Woman, there is no way you're not going to get it tonight. Where there is a will, you can be sure there is a way, and I will find it. You can believe me, there are many ways. You haven't seen anything yet Woman. Wait until we get our own place. I guarantee you will never be allowed out of our bed; your body will be used time and time again."

"I knew you'd have something in mind. I can hardly wait till we have our own place. I'm all for doing anything I can with you and for you, and of course for me."

Cutting off the trail, they worked their way over to the wooded area cautiously, looking this way and that, studying the terrain to make sure they were not being observed. Finding a comfortable spot among a grouping of trees where the road could be seen easily, but not themselves, they encamped for the night. After eating dried fish with nuoc mam, they threw away the hard bread because it was getting moldier, drank a lot of water, and then they made love and snuggled down for the night. Before sleep came to them, they vowed they would find fresh water and have a hot meal sometime the next day.

After they awoke in the morning and stretched their sore muscles from the previous day's jaunt, they heard a noise off to their left as they looked towards the road. Listening closer, they heard a voice that said, "Good morning to you!" When they turned and stared to the left, a voice behind them said the same, "Good morning to you!" As they turned towards the voice, they pulled out their knives and assumed a martial arts stance. The voice then said from their left side, "Good morning to you!" They turned once more, and there was a man a little taller than Van Ba, broad shouldered, and big for a Vietnamese man, standing there. There was a blanket roll across his chest and a bag full of gear hanging from his left shoulder, He looked to be several years younger than Van Ba's age and had dominate almond eyes and a big smile on his face. He wore a wide sash around his waist that held three knives in it. "I am called the Invisible One! I'm very happy to know you two, Van Ba and Mot."

Mot, awed at this man being there, spoke first. "How did you ever find us? We had to leave a day early, and we saw no one. I thought we were on our own."

"Yeah! Answer her you unworthy one!" demanded Van Ba. He was still in his fighting stance with his knife pointed at the man. "Just how in creation did you know where to find us to start with. We have been very careful in our movements, and a final question. How do we know you really are the Invisible One?"

"The answer to your second question is simple: you didn't see me when I was saying, 'Good Morning to you!' I was invisible to you. I am a member of the No Name who remains in good standing, and Nguyen Hai uses me for many difficult tasks because of my martial arts ability, my invisibility when needed, and my dedication to Nguyen Hai, who raised me from a child to be what I am today.

"As to your first question, I was watching Mr. Hu's hovel, and I saw Trung Hai go in. A few minutes later, I saw you enter. When you came out shortly after wearing different clothes, I was concerned. I checked the hovel and found the slaughter. I knew Trung Hai was the culprit. I never trusted him and always thought he would betray us for any reason. I took the bodies and pulled them into the tree line outside the sub-hamlet and cleaned up what I could in the hovel, hoping to give you time to escape. After I checked the hovel you were staying in and found that you had left, I cut across country to find you. I knew the directions Mr. Hu gave you, so I had a pretty good idea of where you would be."

The Invisible One continued. "We do have a slight problem though. There was another man watching you too. He was part of a group of four thugs hovering in the area. The other three were a distance farther down the road. When you left, he went to them. They must have waited for you, but they didn't know about Mr. Hu's instructions for you to turn off at the next right trail. The big surprise was on them instead of you. Mr. Hu didn't tell you about meeting me in secret to discuss your coming because he thought his aide may have betrayed him and informed some bad people. I was to insure your safety.

"I went as fast as my body would let me, and when I got close to you, I saw you enter this wooded area and I followed a little later. I was watching the trail when you two were moaning and groaning in the throes of love, and believe it or not, the four passed by here on the trail. So, they are ahead of us. It's to our advantage that we know they may lie in wait."

Van Ba lowered his knife and relaxed his stance, but he was still cautious of the man. Mot had already done so. He wanted to know what the man meant by saying 'us.' "You used the words 'us' and 'we' in your speech. Are you with someone? Are you joining Mot and I? We believed that you would only observe us from a distance and that you would be too far away and be too late to assist us if we were robbed or assaulted."

"When Mr. Hu learned your route had been compromised, he informed me that I was to meet and accompany you when you opened the instructions. He believed in safety in numbers. Then that idiot Hai changed the plan for us."

Mot queried, "Do you know who the four thugs are? Are they bandits? Are they Nguyen Hai's enemies? Do they know about our mission? Are they a danger to us? For our own peace of mind, we must know these things about them. We have traveled a long, strenuous road to do our duty to the No Name for Nguyen Hai. Each place we go, we get a different story and change of plans. It's nerve wracking and preys on my mind."

"I understand you've had a long, hard journey up to this point. I think they are the No Name's enemies. Mr. Hu thought so too based on information he'd received and believed his man had informed them of what was going to happen. He had me watching them for three days before you came. They seemed a little more organized and disciplined than ordinary bandits, but not quite as much as assassins would be. They seemed prepared for whatever they had planned." He noticed Mot's knife she was still holding at her side.

"Mot! Your knife is rather small." Taking one of his larger knives from his sash, he handed it to Mot. "Give me your small knife and take this larger one. If we are confronted, the smaller one won't do." They exchanged the knives, and Mot nearly cut her finger when she checked its sharpness. She tucked it away and thanked him for his concern. Even though she was proficient in the martial arts and had studied knife fighting a little, she really didn't want to fight with one. Fighting with knives was not her thing, and she hoped she wouldn't have to. She never told anyone, but she was a little squeamish when it came to a lot of blood being spilled. Seeing dead bodies was not her thing either.

The Invisible One saw the hard and moldy bread on the ground and offered, "I know of a sub-hamlet not far from here where you can get some fresh bread and whatever else you need. For now, take some of mine. I have plenty." As he said this, he took some fresh bread from his bag and handed part to Van Ba and part to Mot. As the pair ate the bread and drank water, the man said, "I see your water bladders are almost flat. I found a small creek back in the woods a little. Better refill them while you can." He told

Mot where it was, and she took all three of their bladders and went to find the creek.

The Invisible man asked Van Ba to relate what had transpired in Mr. Hu's hovel. He began telling him of the time they surprised Trung Hai up in the foothills and how he was supposed to be their watcher and protector till they reached Tra Ke #4. Then he explained Trung Hai's rage as he killed Mr. Hu and his aide, and how he wanted to kill him too, take Mot for his own, and receive his own place of glory with Nguyen Hai and the No Name. Finally, Van Ba told the Invisible One about how Trung Hai lunged at him with his knife and died for the attempt. He explained searching everything in the hovel and changing into other clothes. Van Ba then thanked him for moving the bodies and giving them more time to escape, then continued.

"We didn't trust Tran Hai completely. We stayed on alert and checked behind us when we could. For some unknown reason, he just didn't seem right. I wasn't really surprised when I saw him in Mr. Hu's hovel with the murdered ones." Van Ba went on, "He had sworn he was our protection! Ha! Our protection my ass. What really made me mad was how he talked about Mot. Even if he hadn't killed them, I would have killed him over those remarks he made. No one will ever speak like that about Mot within my hearing."

He continued, "I'm worried about Mot fighting if we have to. Martial arts come easy for her, but she may be pregnant with my baby! I don't want her or the baby to get hurt. We plan to marry at the end of this mission."

"We'll protect her as much as possible I assure you, and not just because she's a woman, but because she's a valuable asset to the No Name also. I want you to know too that I don't believe in anyone hurting women either. If I'm there, the one who does so will feel my wrath too." Van Ba indicated he felt the same way.

Mot returned announcing she was back, and she was smiling as she walked up with the full water bladders. Van Ba thought she looked beautiful. The Invisible One told her, "I'm glad you found the creek and you found your way back. We need a plan of attack in case we are confronted along the way."

"There are four of them, so this is what I propose. I will scout ahead in secret from time to time, and if I find them, I'll try to get us around them unseen. And if we must confront them, Mot, you take on the smallest one. Van Ba you start with the biggest. I'll take on the other two. I'll fight with two of my knives. When I've finished them off, I will take the bigger one from you, and you can help Mot if she needs it. If they are ordinary bandits, they won't be good fighters, but if they are enemies of the No Name, they may have trained a little and have some fighting skills. I don't think they will know that we are very good at martial arts until it's too late. Yes, I know you two are good; Mr. Hu told me of your skills. I hope that we can take one of them alive and that he's willing to talk. If he's not willing to talk, I'm sure we can find a way to loosen his tongue. We need to know if there will be others after us and the Jade Cross and where they may be located. I don't think they would know about the sealed letter or what your package is because the aide didn't know either, but they will want the package."

Van Ba and Mot hesitantly agreed with him and vowed to do their best if they needed to fight. They would give no quarter nor expect anything else towards them. Above all, the Jade Cross and the sealed letter must get to Nguyen Hai regardless of what might happen to them. After relieving themselves, the trio packed up and started walking across the field to the trail, being ever vigilant. Although they were close together, they didn't clasp arms, but they did look like they were walking down a new road towards a new adventure.

After a short walk, they came to an area of higher ground, possibly a low outcrop or a small part of the foothills. The trail followed the curve of the high ground, and they could not see around it. The Invisible One told them, "The sub-hamlet I referred to is a short distance up the trail around this outcrop. You two sit here and rest your weary bones while I go over this high ground and scout ahead. Maybe I'll check out the sub-hamlet too, if it is warranted. We don't need to be surprised by our enemies on the way to it. I'll be back shortly." With that declaration, he moved up the high ground.

The lovers moved off of the trail and part way up the rise, put their loads on the ground, sat down, and hugged each other tight and kissed a few times. Then they drank from the bladders, leaned back against their loads, and rested but kept on the alert. Danger could come from the part of the trail that couldn't be seen or from behind the high ground. Although they were not totally afraid, they were very apprehensive sitting there and not knowing what might be happening with the Invisible One. The unknown could always prey on one's mind.

Their main concern at this point was how they would fare if anything happened with the Invisible One and they had no support or back up.

CHAPTER 7

The Invisible One came back in no time. "The trail is clear going into the sub hamlet. To be safe though, let me go into it a little ahead of you. I can look around and make sure it's clear. When I see you come, I will wave you off if there is danger, otherwise come straight in. We'll go straight to the small market and get you fresh bread and whatever else you need. He took a drink of water and he headed off to the sub hamlet. Van Ba and Mot waited for about fifteen minutes and then made their way slowly into the sparsely populated area. As promised the Invisible One was waiting for them close to a hovel with a calm look on his face and waving them on. He led them to the market place.

They shopped and talked to venders, bought fresh bread, a little more rice, fresh vegetables and some more tea. They were enjoying the moment because there had not been much leisurely activity during their trek. As the trio started to leave the Invisible One stopped them. "Look at that man with the bedroll and bag walking up the path. That's the one who was watching Mr. Hu's hovel. You two keep shopping and talking and I'm going to follow him and see where he's going. They may be waiting for us outside of this sub hamlet. If I'm not back in an hour or two go back the way we came in and move up onto the high ground and try to hide. If you have to go there, I will find you." He was off, going around the market and exiting the backside of the sub-hamlet.

Mot and Van Ba both felt the same way. Mot was the first to say it. "What happens if we are up there and he doesn't come back? What if he's caught and those guys force him to tell where we are and kill him? Do we backtrack and take a different route now?"

"Those are good points Mot. I don't know the answers. We'll have to wait and see, then make our own plans. Our friend seems to be very able to handle things. He's very intelligent, dedicated, and is a very staunch individual. I don't believe he would talk about us if he was captured. But, then, you never know about those things. There are those who are very good at torture during their interrogations. Let's keep our fingers crossed and hope that doesn't happen to him." They continued to stroll around the market looking over foods and goods and talking with the vendors.

"Van Ba, I've been thinking about something important to me and I hope important to you too. What will we name our child if it's a girl? What name to we give to a boy? Think on it please! Then, let me know what you think about it."

"I hadn't thought of that. I will think hard on it when I get the chance."

The Invisible One caught sight of the man just outside the sub hamlet. The guy was walking towards a wooded area and didn't see the Invisible one move quickly around to back of it and enter the tree line. When the Invisible One saw there were no others in the woods, he moved parallel to the man and before they were past the woods, he jumped the man from behind without warning, threw him down to the ground and had his knee pressed into the man's midsection just under the ribs and one of his knives pressed to his throat. The man was terrified thinking this was a bandit and was going to rob him of his possessions and kill him.

"What do you want of me?" he said as his urine soaked his pants. "I'm just a poor peasant who has nothing to give and I want to live."

"Here's the deal. I'm not here to rob you or to kill you! I know what you are. I've watched you and your friends for a few days. I'm going to ask you some very important questions I need answers to, and if you do not answer them your head may leave your body very quickly. Do you understand me?"

"Yes! I understand" The man responded weekly, afraid to move a muscle.

"Why were you watching Mr. Hu's hovel?"

"I was being paid to watch for someone getting a package from Chinaman, a Mr. Hu and report it to a gang leader. When I saw the two people leave with the package, I left Tra Ke #4 and reported it."

"Who paid you to do this watching?"

"It was Nguyen Tam, the one who gives orders to the others."

"How many others are there?"

"There are only two more men with him." The Invisible one already knew this but asked it as a control question so as to learn if the man was being truthful.

"Who do they work for?"

"I swear to Buda, I don't know who they work for. I never heard it said. I was pulled from my hovel in Tra Ke #4 three weeks ago and told to help them spy on the sub-hamlet or else, and I would be paid handsomely if they had success in their mission. The leader gave me a few Dong in advance."

"I see. So, if you were forced to help them by spying on Mr. Hu, then why are you still staying with those three men and what are their plans for the two travelers?" the Invisible One inquired of the man.

"I was told that if I didn't stay with them, in case I was needed to spy even more, I would be beaten very badly and left beside the road with no pay. After the man and woman left Tra Ke #4 by a different trail and didn't pass by them I was told I would be used to look for them in any sub hamlet we may pass through. I think they want to kill the two, after raping the woman and taking the package, whatever it is. That's all I know." The man was really very afraid and trembling now. His pants seemed to get wetter in the crotch area.

"Why were you in this sub hamlet if they are up ahead?"

"Nguyen Tam sent me to check the sub hamlet and see if the two travelers were in it because he didn't know if the two were up ahead or behind us, and report back to him soon. I didn't see them so I was on my way to report back to him and hope he would pay me and let me return to my home. Believe me! I've never done anything bad in my life."

"Where are the three now, and, are they waiting in ambush?"

"They're down the road about fifteen minutes away from here. They're in a small clearing close to the trail on the right-hand side. They are waiting to jump the two travelers with their knives if they should come by there. I don't know anything else about them or what else they are up to. I've only been a paid and frightened stooge for them. I'm just a poor and lonely farmer's helper that works hard in the dry rice fields; I work day in and day out. My family is old and they need me to support them. They have no one else to help them. Are you going to kill me now?"

The Invisible One smiled at the man and asked, "Let me ask you this question. Do you know of the Invisible One and his feats?"

"I have heard of him, he's a great warrior," the man gulped with tears beginning to form in his eyes. "Please make it quick! I'm a coward, I hate to be hurt, and I don't want to suffer when you do it."

"I am the Invisible one. This is your Lucky day. I only kill in self-defense or for the good of the No Name Society. You pose no threat to me or the two travelers, so I've no desire to harm you the least bit. When I let you get up, I want you to return to Tra Ke #4 as quickly as possible and never talk about this whole situation with anyone. If you do, I will come for you. Do you understand me?"

"Oh, yes, Invisible one. In gratitude for my life, I will always do as you ask. My family and I will always pray for your well-being."

The Invisible One reached inside his tunic and took out a wad of money. He peeled off 30 Dong and gave it to the man. "This is for your discomfort at my hands and your good information. I hope you have a good long life. Take care of your family." The man looked at the dong and couldn't believe his good fortune. Invisible One let the man up, patted him on the back. The man bowed with his palms together and in front of his face and thanked him over and over for his life then turned and started running toward his home. The Invisible One gave him a slight head start then went to the sub hamlet, keeping the man in his sight to make sure he left for his home, and to meet with his companions.

Van Ba and Mot, from their spot by the market place entrance saw the man pass close by and feared the worst for the Invisible One. Mot wanted to leave right away fearing that the men could be coming for them. Van Ba put his arm around her shoulders and whispered, "I don't think he even saw us. Let's wait a few more minutes and wander away slowly. We don't want to draw attention to ourselves. Besides, it looks like that guy's pants were wet in the front. I think we don't have to worry about our friend at all. Let's have a bit of faith in him."

"I sure hope your right. I do trust your judgment Van Ba. If I'm with your baby I don't want either of us to be hurt." Van Ba agreed.

Van Ba released her and stepped onto the path from the market entrance and saw their new found friend entering at the far end of the sub hamlet. He stepped back close to Mot, pulled her hair aside, placed his lips next to her ear and whispered that their guy was coming. Then he stuck his tongue in her ear and wiggled it. She shivered from head to toe. Van Ba was delighted to say the least.

The three greeted each other and walked from the sub hamlet in silence at the Invisible One's request. When they were past the last hovel the Invisible One brought them up to date. "With only three guys to worry about now it could be easier to counter their ambush. After we pass the wooded area up the road on the right, you pause for a while, giving me some time, then move on up the road."

I'll circle around through the field to the clearing and get behind them. When you come upon a clearing along the right side of the path and close to it, approach it casually as you would normally. When you're confronted, I'll attack them from behind. One of them is named Nguyen Tam, the man who is in charge. I hope we can take him alive. He'll have many answers that we need."

"That sounds like a good plan to me," Van Ba stated. He looked at Mot and smiled. "Mot, when we're confronted you take out your knife for show only, but stay a several steps behind me. Our friend and I can take them. Invisible

One, can we just slash up their legs a bit? It would keep Nguyen Tam alive."

"I was told you were very wise as well as being a good fighter. The legs it is. We can decide what to do with them after we get some answers. If things don't go the way we want we may have to kill them. Will you and Mot be all right with that?"

"Mot and I will do whatever necessary to complete our mission, deliver the Jade Cross and the letter successfully and safely to Nguyen Hai. I've never wished to kill, but I have done so when needed and had no regrets about it." Mot moved her head up and down in agreement. The trio was now walking along the wooded area growing close to its end.

"We're at the point I must leave you from. Sit here and rest a bit. When I moved through the woods to confront the spy, I noticed a stream in the woods. You can refresh your water supply. Don't worry about taking too much time as I must find the best way to get behind them unseen. See you there, friends." The man waved to them and began jogging through the field at a quick pace.

Mot dropped her load and helped Van Ba with his. She kissed his cheek then took the water bladders in to the woods to find the stream. When she returned, they drank deeply from one bladder then Mot took it back to the stream and refilled it. Returning again, she sat against her man and he held her tight. She really liked being in his arms. She had never thought she could ever enjoy any man as she did Van Ba. She also never in her life ever expected to do the things she and her man were doing with any man as she had thought those things were vile and disgusting. She was in seventh heaven when she was held like this. It was a comfort to her that she had never known before meeting Van Ba. After a few minutes they laid back and nodded off for a while.

Mot, as usual, woke up first and elbowed her man gently in the ribs and telling him, with a smile, to wake his butt up, especially if he wanted to do something later on, like get some butt. He shook his head to rid his sleepiness and smiled down at her and kissed her gently. Responding she returned the kiss harder, deeper and more meaning full. "Mot, you're lucky we have to leave here now or you'd really get it. I've never known a woman who could make me so damned horny before." Mot grinned and groped him then she started toward the trail.

"Van Ba, you are so stupid some times. That makes me very unlucky, you dummy." She grabbed his manhood hard again then stood up. She had big grin on her face. He thought she was precious. He knew it was nice to have a horny woman.

They were loaded up and started up the trail once more, walking at their normal pace and acting as natural as possible. When they saw the clearing, Van Ba reminded her to stay a few paces behind him as a Vietnamese woman would. He told her that when and if she was confronted by any one of the thugs to only fight if she needed to protect herself. She knew she would fight if Van Ba looked like he needed help whether he liked it or not. He was her man and no ass would ever cause harm to him.

The three men hiding in the clearing were wondering what happened to their spy. "That coward must have run back home. He should have been back long ago. You just can't rely on or trust those kinds of namby, pamby, peasants," Nguyen Tam complained. Then he noticed the travelers coming up the path and alerted his men to get ready.

Van Ba and Mot were close to the near edge of the clearing when the three men with knives drawn ran from it, placing their selves about ten feet in front of and directly in the couple's path. The pair drew their knives and assumed fighting stances, and slowly Mot, after she had drawn her knife, moved several feet behind her protector taking a fighting stance as Van Ba had told her to do.

The Man in the middle demanded of Van Ba and Mot, "You vagabonds just drop your loads where you stand and go back to the sub-hamlet and we'll let you live, well, maybe we will!"

"Do you really expect us to believe you'll let us live if we do? You just don't want to get blood on the bags when you kill us. We'll drop our loads, but it will be so we can fight unburdened by them." He and Mot carefully removed their loads and set them aside. "By the way, which of you is Nguyen Tam? I heard he was a low life sniveling ass, that kisses water buffalos' dicks." This took the men by surprise that the leader's name was known, and they looked at each other in a puzzled manner. Van Ba saw the Invisible One slip from inside the clearing moving quietly towards the men's backs.

The man in the middle raised his hand and declared, "I am Nguyen Tam. I don't care for your insults and now we are going to cut you to ribbons and take your package. Your leader will never see it. Then we will have fun with your woman. I know she'll want more of our affections before we finish you off completely. You'll get to watch the fun and games as your last breath leaves your' body. Then we'll kill her too, get rid of your' bodies and no one will ever know what happened to you two."

Before the two of the men could move towards their prey the man to the right of Nguyen Tam started to move towards Van Ba, his knife thrust forward, then screamed and collapsed. The Invisible one had thrown one of his knives in to the man's lower back piercing vital organs. As the other two men looked behind to see what had happened Van Ba did a front shoulder roll at the man on the leader's left, came up and with a précised motion slashing his hamstring. The man also fell to the ground in pain and dropped his knife to grab at his thigh, spurting blood. Nguyen Tam looked front and back at his two advisories that were in fighting stances with their knives pointed at him, decided cowardice was the better part of valor, dropped his knife and sank to his knees, begging that his life be spared.

Acting spontaneously Mot quickly cut two strips of cloth from her oldest blanket and rushed to stem the bleeding of the wounded man's thigh. She tied one tightly above the wound and the other over and around the wound, told the man to lie still and went to check the other wounded one. Turning him over she could see his eyes were becoming glassy and his face was becoming ashen with a trickle of blood coming from his lips. She placed her hand over his heart but could not feel a hear beat. She knew the guy wouldn't make it, so she pulled the knife from his back, walked to the side of the road, wiped the blood on the grass and then returned the knife to its owner.

The Invisible One pulled a rope from his pack, cut off a small length and tied Nguyen Tam's hands behind him. He cut another length and tied the other man's hands too. The guy was moaning and groaning over his wound so he asked Mot to cut another piece of cloth and stuff it in the guy's mouth. She was happy to do so. His screams had been screeching and piercing in her ears. Now it was muffled and not as maddening to the ears.

Nguyen Tam was still on his knees and Van Ba reached over, grabbed his right ear and twisted it hard forcing the man's head to the left side causing him to give a yelp. "Now tell me what you're going to do with my woman and you'll be a eunuch before you know it. The last bastard who threatened to harm her is gone from this world. Before he died, she made sure he left this world without his balls and male member. She loves to cut them off of turds and shove them in their mouths."

The Invisible One quickly placed a hand on Van Ba's shoulder and reminded him in a soft voice, but one Nguyen Tam could hear, that they needed to ask some questions first, then Van Ba could do as he liked to this unworthy one, even castration. Mot surprised them by saying, "I'd like to do that to him too. Also, his pitiful friend."

The Invisible One looked sternly at Nguyen Tam as Van Ba released the ear. "If you are going to ambush someone you should learn how to cover your ass first. This kind of crap only pisses people like us, off. I haven't yet decided how I want to motivate you to talk. There are so many ways. I could beat you with my fists, or a club, but then maybe you could withstand that. Maybe I could break many of your bones. That could make you pass out and you would be useless to question. There is also the death of a thousand cuts. I just start with small cuts here and there on your body when you don't answer a question to my satisfaction. I might even do several small cuts when you don't respond. Eventually you'll bleed to death." While speaking to the man he cut another length of rope, stepped behind the still kneeling man and tied the ankles together. He walked away and motioned the lovers over for a chat letting Nguyen Tam think about his fate.

"You two have acted as I knew you would. You've great courage and I'm proud to be with you. Van Ba, I knew you wouldn't give me away while I snuck up behind them. Now we must concentrate on the two prisoners. I'm sure the wounded man heard what I told the big shit. We'll leave them stew in their own juices for a while before we question them. Mot, check the guy's wound again and try to stop more bleeding while your partner helps me carry the dead one into the clearing and cover him over with dirt and leaves."

Mot cut another strip of blanket and tied it tightly above the other one, stemming the blood flow some more then checked the gag in his mouth to make sure he wasn't choking since he'd quieted down some. Just for good measure she kicked him in the balls then moved to the kneeling one and did the same. She stepped back and waited for the others to return, and keeping an eye on Nguyen Tam. Pointing her knife at him she informed Tam, "You're very lucky right now. I'd have no problem castrating you this very instance." She moved to his side and backhanded him across the nose, drawing blood. She stepped back, stared at him and waited for the men to return. "Since you're tied up and you can't do it yourself, I guess I'd have to cut your pants off first. Ugh! I don't really want to touch your scummy pants, but I would.

When the men returned from the clearing the three sat down at the side of the road in the grass under the shade the trees offered, drank some water and ate bread, making sure the prisoners could see them. They talked, joked and laughed while pretending not to care about the plight of their captives sitting on the path in the sun that was beating down on them. Soon it would be time to start the questions.

"One thing that concerns me is that these guys were clumsy. Real pros or good bandits would have jumped all over you without talking and we would have had a big fight to cope with. That could mean there may be others who are better waiting somewhere in case these guys failed to get the cross."

The Invisible One thought a minute and continued, "That could also mean that someone knows you two are very smart and capable of getting around these guys. That would also mean there has to be a spy near Nguyen Hai if my thinking is correct. I hope these two have the answers. I guess it's time to start my interrogation technique. Let's have a go and take a shot at it."

The Invisible One walked over to Nguyen Tam and pulled out the short knife he had gotten from Mot. He checked it for sharpness with his thumb and stared directly into the bound man's eyes. "I've decided how to question you." He let his words sink into the man's mind and he could both see and smell the guy's fear. His cracked lips were trembling and his body quivered. He was ripe for questioning. The front of his pants suddenly became wet and smelly from his urine and tears rolled down his cheeks. Van Ba wondered if he would crap in his pants too.

The Invisible One cut off part of one of the man's lower pant leg and without a word placed the knife edge along his calf. Then, he spoke to the man softly. "Your friend will have trouble walking with a bad limp the rest of his life due to his thigh injury. The same could be said of an individual who has a like injury to his calf muscle. Would people laugh at you for hobbling around your sub hamlet? Most likely they would. They would think you were a dummy. I don't think my knife, actually its Mot's knife, is as sharp as I need it to be." He rose, walked a few feet away, took a small stone from his pocket and began to hone the knife to a keener edge, smiling at the man the whole time.

After honing the knife, the Invisible One moved to the Nguyen Tam, stooped down and broke the skin of his calf with a light slash of the knife. There was only a light trickle of blood flowing, but it did the trick. Seeing his own blood and crying loudly, more tears running down his face, he pleaded, "Don't cut me anymore! I'll tell you what ever I know! Just ask me. Please don't hurt me anymore!"

"If you don't want more pain than you can handle, then you must be truthful. One thing for you to consider is that you do not know how much I already know." He stood and walked to the tree line and picked up a thick stick. Walked back to Nguyen Tam and cut the stick easily in to two pieces with his sharp knife, and showed them to the man. He had decided to start with questions to recent events which he knew the answers to test the man's veracity. Now he would ask his first question.

"Did you and your gang kidnap a man from his hovel in Tra Ke #4 a few nights ago?"

He gulped and answered, "Yes!"

"Why did you do this to that man?"

"We needed someone to spy for us."

"Did you promise to pay him for spying and if so, how much?"

"Yes! I promised him 15 Dong if he did a good job and I gave him a few Dong to make him believe me."

"Tell me what he was to spy on and why?

"We needed him to watch the hovel of a Mr. HU, a Chinaman pretending to be Vietnamese, and report back to us immediately if some guy left Mr. Hu's hovel with some kind of a package."

"What kind of a package is it and what is in it?"

"All we knew was it was some kind of a package, but not what was in it." So far so good, thought the Invisible One.

"Why didn't you just go in and rob and kill Mr. Hu?

"I was instructed that getting the package was very important and must be kept secret so no one would know what happened to it and make sure the bearer of it was never seen again. Mr. Hu nor his aide, who was our informant, was not to be harmed."

Now he would begin more pointed questions. "How did you know that a Chinaman would have an important package in his hovel?"

"A strange man with a plain white mask on came to our sub hamlet along the Red River and hired us to do it."

"Why did he choose you three to do it?"

"We had a reputation for robbery, assault, and rape throughout several hamlet areas. The masked one knew we had been forced from a few hamlet complexes for our crimes and he felt we wouldn't hesitate to retrieve the package and kill the bearer of it. He promised to pay us when we delivered the package to him"

"Do you know who that man is?"

"No! Never saw him before. He only assured us that that this deed was to the betterment of our country."

"Where were you to deliver it?"

"He told us to go towards our sub hamlet and we would be contacted along the way by some messenger."

"Have you ever heard of the No Name and how they treat those who oppose or cross the society?"

"You don't mean that I've done a disservice to the No Name, do you?" The Invisible one moved his head up and down. "You're going to kill me now, aren't you?"

The Invisible One didn't answer that question. He only said, "I must go over and speak with my friends. They may have more questions for you. I know that I will have more questions after that." Always leave the prisoner with the thought that you weren't through with him and that there was still more to come. He walked over to Van Ba and Mot with a grin that Nguyen Tam could not see.

The man was crying harder and shivered harder in terror. The other gang member was now passed out from shock.

To Van Ba, and Mot he mentioned, "Let's eat more bread and drink water and let them see us enjoying our feast and having a good time. Those two are probably getting hungry and thirsty by now, even though the wounded one has passed out. The promise of food and drink may get us more answers later. These guys are only tough when they have the upper hand. By the way Mot, speaking of a hand, it looks like one must have accidentally hit him in the face while we hid the body."

Mot giggling replied, "Is that so. I wonder who would be ornery enough to do something like that to such an adored and respected person, and also threaten him with castration. Maybe there is another Invisible One around, a female one."

The two men laughed and laughed.

CHAPTER 8

Mот told the others that the two turds were watching their every bite that they took. The wounded one had regained some consciousness and was grunting a low moan. Soon he and the other one would need water and food. So, in addition to the bread they took out some dried fish and nuoc mam and ate even more heartedly. She didn't know why but she felt good that these men who would have robbed and harmed or killed her man and raped and killed her, were suffering and now wanted food and water. She hoped they starved to death after she castrated them. She also knew Van Ba and the Invisible One wouldn't let her do that, although they might do it themselves. Standing up she showed them a water bladder and took a drink from it, poured a little on the ground, waved the water bladder at them and sat back down.

The Invisible One told her, "You'd make a good interrogator Mot. You can project yourself as a heartless bitch. You've got the good moves to get into a guy's inner self with your beauty and your' brains. Guys like them have no respect for any of the women they meet or how they treat their bodies and a woman like you can use that against them easily." She nodded her head in thanks for the compliment and smiled at him with an upturn of her lips. She hadn't realized she had used an interrogation approach technique.

While chatting away they made plans for their evening stop and fare. They'd have boiled rice, vegetables, and most importantly, having hot tea would be a treat. Making this decision was easy. Now it was time for more answers and deciding what to do with the two captives. Just killing them now as opposed to offing them in combat wasn't their thing.

They cleaned up their small messes they made with the food and approached the two, as Mot called them, useless turds. Van Ba stopped, thought, and tapped them on the shoulders and beckoned them to follow him into the clearing. Out of ear shot of the two useless turds he said, "We need to find where their gear is stashed and go through it before we ask any more questions. There could be good information hidden in it. We need as much knowledge as we can obtain in order to complete our journey safely."

"Good thinking partner," the Invisible One commented. "I inadvertently let this one item slip by me," the Invisible One lamented. "I should have done that search the first thing."

"Not really. If he has lied to us and there's something for us to find out, it'll prey on their minds if they know your searching through their gear. Mot, you help our friend search their gear and I'll watch the prisoners. I'll tell them you're searching their gear then I'll just stand and grin at them." He did just that. Grinning and staring at them after he told them about the search, made him feel good inside because he knew they were hurting now and the grinning would drive them bonkers. If they had half the chance, they would do the same shit to him and to Mot, and even worse.

Returning from the copse the two brought out the turd's gear and placed it where the two rogues could see it. They slowly took everything out of the bags and blanket rolls, making sure the two turds were watching their every move they made. Mot handed her guys a note she found in one of the blanket rolls and stated. "When I found this note in the blanket roll I knew we had them figuratively by the balls for sure. Now we just need to cut them off one at a time and that other thing too." Van Ba and the Invisible One laughed heartedly at Mot. She was getting to be a quite character. Van Ba read the note to his self then read it aloud to the others. They then agreed that this note gave them one answer at least.

> *Nguyen Tam*
>
> *Everything is arranged as we planned. After you get the package, do not open it, and do not leave any witnesses, including your men. Somewhere along your route back to your sub-hamlet, a man, Trich Tuy, will contact you and you will give him the package. He will pay you well when you meet. You are doing a great service on our behalf.*
>
> *Your humble patriot*
> *Nguyen Phat*

Van Ba moved to the man on his knees and held the paper in front of him then held it in front of the other guy. He faced them both, saying, "Do you tell us about these people now, what else you know about them and get food and drink, or do I just let Mot cut your balls off. She'll do it too. She's a very mean and vindictive woman. You're lucky you didn't have to fight her. I have to put up with her every day of the year and I know of no man who can defeat her. She is very skilled at all of the martial arts, especially with a knife. I've seen her skin men alive before she kills them. That's just part of her version of death by a thousand cuts. I want you two to think about it for a while."

With that said to the two bandits, he walked away from them and sat beside Mot, who was patiently sharpening her knife, and was grinning at them anew. Mot slid closer to him and said in his ear, "You really poured it on my man. I can see they are ready to talk, but they need to stew a little while longer, I think. Van Ba, I don't do the death by a thousand cuts," she whispered to him, "but I might do death by a thousand bites on a certain part of your body." She put her face into his shoulder where the turds couldn't see her face and blushed. It was hard for him not to show any reaction to her while grinning at the turds.

The Invisible One scooted over and the three put their heads together and decided the next course of action. The Invisible one would ask questions, Van Ba would continue grinning at them, and Mot would sharpen her knife where the two guys could still see her. She began her knife sharpening anew and the turds looked more scared of her than of the guys.

Nguyen Tam looked worse than the wounded guy. The invisible One thought that the reason he and the other two were chosen was because they were weak minded and expendable. Not for their manliness, that was one thing for sure. The Invisible Man's first question was, "What do you know about Nguyen Phat?"

Tam's lips were dried out and cracking and with a hoarse voice asked, "Water please. Give me water and I'll tell you everything." The Invisible One looked at Van Ba and he brought a water bladder over. He tilted the man's head back and dripped some water on his lips. Start telling your story and you'll get a good drink. With a lick of his wet lips Tam began.

"I've known Nguyen Phat for years. When we first became friends, we worked for a bandit near Hanoi. We robbed, raped and murdered throughout several sub-hamlets in the Hanoi vicinity for about three or four years.

We finely left the bandit, Phat went his way and I went mine. He told me he was going to work for a group that hated that No Name bunch to no end. That was the last time I saw him until he found me a few weeks ago. He explained that he had an important job to be handled by someone he could trust, asked me and my pals to work for him. I agreed and he said he would keep in contact until time to put the plan into action."

"After having three meetings to get reacquainted with him he told us about a Mr. Hu in Tra Ke #4 and that I must retrieve a package given to some man by him. He said nothing about the woman being with him. He said it was time and sent us off. We were about three quarters there when a man found us and verified Mr. Hu and an aide were now in Tra Ke #4 and that the man who sought Mr. HU had a woman with him to feed and service him. He told us about the man and the woman's capabilities and how they performed on the way to Tra Ke #4. I asked him how he knew this and he said he had tried to rob them and the woman kicked him in the head knocking him out and when he woke up the man did it too. That's all I know, period. You already know the rest."

Van Ba held the water bladder to him and he drank greedily. Van Ba knew that at some point when you're interrogating someone you need to keep small promises to keep the interrogation on track and the prisoner cooperating. Van Ba turned to the other guy and gave him a drink too.

"You heard what your friend told the Invisible One, is that the truth," Van Ba queried. The guy nodded and moaned a soft yes. "I think you should know you are very lucky today. I usually kill rather than wound. It could have been much worse for you. Remember this! You will live if we so decide."

"Oh shit!" Nguyen Tam moaned and looked over at Van Ba's friend. "You are the Invisible One for real?"

"That I am. You've heard of me?"

"I've heard many stories of your deeds. I know Nguyen Phat considered you an enemy because of your work with the No Name and being raised by Nguyen Hai. I think he was afraid of you the way he talked. I know I damn sure am. He warned us that we should be careful lest we run into you. Please tell me, is she really that crazy. Will she really cut my balls off?"

"Answer a few more questions for me and I'll talk to her in your favor. Why did you kidnap that man in Tra Ke #4 and make him work for you." This one knows everything about the situation Nguyen Tam was thinking, so he must not lie to him. Maybe he could bargain for his life. He wasn't worried about his sidekick's well-being.

"We didn't want to cause suspicion among the dwellers there by wondering in and out of there a few days in a row. It was reasonable that any person living there could move around without anyone noticing. Also, he could get us needed supplies from the market easier and cheaper than we could." So, we decided to grab a local guy and intimidate him to work for us."

"Did you intend to kill him when you were through using him as a spy?"

"Yes!"

"Were you going to kill Mr. Hu and his aide also?"

"No! We were strictly ordered not to harm them because it could cause trouble for us with the people there. Trouble like that we didn't need. Besides, those two were not really involved in any of the No Name's operations."

"Do you think your friend Nguyen Phat would go so far as to have you and your men murdered after you turned over the package?"

No! We've been good friends for a long time. He wouldn't do that to me, ever."

"You're dumber than I thought, just like that rock laying there on the path. Think hard about it! Didn't he tell you to leave no witnesses or something like that?

"Yes! But you think he would kill us?'

"I know he would. You are a witness and he's a very ruthless man and has probably done worse things than you ever could. After his man got the package from you, you were dead meat. You may not realize it, but the No Name serves the country by ferreting out its enemies and destroying them before they can do harm to the country. We are the good guys. Your friend Nguyen Phat will rob and murder for any reason, we don't. No matter what you've heard we don't kill anyone unless we absolutely have to. Our women don't cut balls off either unless forced to. You should know though that the woman is a martial arts expert. I'd never want to fight her. I need to talk to my friends now, but first I'll pull you and your friend into the shade of the trees and shortly, if we think you were truthful, we'll give you both some food and more water."

"Mot, would you go through their gear and get out their food and water. They really need to be hydrated and fed, and I want them to relax and regain a little strength and trust us before I send them back to the sub—hamlet we passed through. After they eat there's one more question I must ask. I think one or the other will be more than willing to answer it."

The three took the guys' food and water to them, unbound the pair's hands and let them eat and drink. The water was the first thing they gulped down. Then they attacked their bread, dried fish and nuoc mam like starved animals. When they finished their meal the Invisible One addressed them anew.

"We need to know if either of you have any idea just where this guy is supposed to meet and retrieve the package from you. It could be an ambush set up to get the package and then kill you, leaving no witnesses. We can surprise them as we did you if we know about where it is and you help us by giving us that information."

The wounded one answered, "I think it was near a sub-hamlet named Ap Bac #2. I'm not quite sure where it is yet."

Nguyen Tam continued with, "I know where it is. Ap Bac is a main hamlet of a large village with three large hamlets about ten miles before you reach the Red River. It's only about a two days journey from here. There are plenty of wooded areas and streams between here and there. Trich Tuy could be anywhere along the route. I wasn't to know exactly where he would be because the location of the meet could change at any time do to any reason, but Phat told me that the guy named Trich Tuy would find me."

"You have been very cooperative and truthful to us so your life and the life of your companion are spared, but you must agree to my terms before we release you, first. I do not say this in a boastful manner. I am a very serious person."

"Oh yes! Yes! We'll do anything you ask. We'll pledge our lives to you." They spoke almost in unison as though they had been practicing the words for hours.

The Invisible One addressed both guys. "Nguyen Tam, you help your man back to the last sub-hamlet and get him help for his wound and care for him until it's healed. Then you two must learn to work in the fields as honest men. You're never to rob or rape again, ever. I have friends in that sub-hamlet and if you don't change your robbing and raping ways, I will know about it and come after you and I will not spare your life again. You're never to go to Tra Ke #4 again for any reason. Mr. Hu and his aide were murdered there, not by us, this skilled man here, Van Ba, killed their attacker, and I'm sure the people there would like to get someone for it when they find their bodies and make them pay dearly for their deed. I sent your spy back there with instructions to tell the people you did it if you should return there. Last, if I need a favor from you in the future you will do as I say. Do the two of you understand and agree to these terms?"

Both guys heartily agreed to his terms. They were given theirs' and the dead man's gear, water, and food. Van Ba even lopped off and trimmed a pair of tree limbs to be used as crutches for the wounded one. The Invisible One threw two of their knives as far up the trail in the sub hamlet's direction as he could for them to pick up on their way as they may need them for some protection or as a simple tool.

After the two robbers gave thanks to the trio and bowed to the trio while pledging their lives to the Invisible One, their feet were untied. The three companions headed on their way leaving the two guys behind them struggling on up the road.

Mot looked at her lover and asked, "I wonder what it would have been like to have cut off their balls? Especially to castrate the mouthy one! He really pissed me off big time." The two men laughed at this and Van Ba, quipped, "That's my woman. I hope she never changes."

Smiling he added, "I hope she doesn't ever get mad at me while I'm sleeping! However, If she castrated me it would cut off her night time snacks!" He laughed heartily. Giggling, Mot slapped him behind the head and mentioned to him that he'd better not piss her off. She had a knife and could find night time snacks elsewhere.

Traveling the rest of the day was arduous at times. It was getting to the point where it became one step at a time. Carrying their gear, sweating, and feeling the fatigue of their long journey even in the cool early spring weather, where they now were, was becoming a problem and they coped with it as well as they could. At times they were silent, at times they would talk about whatever came into their heads, and sometimes they spoke of their predicament and made what little plans they could. They saw a couple of sub-hamlets off in the distance along the way with narrow paths leading to them and famers on their buffalos. Much of the countryside was beautiful even though the season was still cool. Before long there would be a monsoon season in parts of the country and they were heading in that direction. Collectively they hoped they would beat the rains to their destination.

If they had to pass wooded areas close to the trail the Invisible one would scout ahead. A cool stream was found and the water bladders were refilled and their faces washed. Just before sundown they found a nice thicket with a good camping area within, built a cooking fire and settled in for the night. Mot fixed a hot meal of rice, vegetables, bread and tea and this time there were no leftovers. Van Ba and the Invisible One took turns standing guard during the night. The sun was already up an hour before they were awake and refreshed. They ate dried fish and bread with hot tea for breakfast, geared up and resumed their travel.

Up the trail they began to talk about the hamlet Ap Bac and how to approach it. Mot said she had been the guide for a group that went through Ap Bac one time. She told the guys that she would try to remember as much as she could about the place, but they must give her time to think. It had been a couple of years since she passed by there as she began as a guide at a young age. The Invisible One proposed that he didn't really want to scout that area, but he would if they got to close to it, because he could be easily spotted and recognized. He would leave far enough ahead of the group as to make a good and safe recon.

They had an uneventful day traveling except for aching bodies. They could feel the burn in their feet, and especially the legs. They passed peasants on the road, did some sightseeing, and settled in a large wooded area for the night. The Invisible One asked of Mot what she remembered about the sub-hamlet, Ap Bac #2.

"Ap Bac #2 is part of Son Binh Village which has five Hamlet complexes. It's the largest village we will pass through before reaching our destination. The Village headquarters has a very large market place where you can get anything you need. There is a lot of dry farmed rice and vegetable farming around the area. The Village is drier than the Red River Basin area, where wet rice is grown in the paddies formed by dykes, and that begins about a day and a half trek or so south east of there. The Red River starts in Yunnan, China, and flows to the Red River Delta where it empties into the gulf of Tonkin. (It gets its name and color due to the large amount of silt it carries which is rich in iron oxide.) Unless an ambush is to take place in or around one of the sub-hamlets around Ap Bac I can't think of any place they could hide and ambush us because the area is very flat and it leads to the flood plains, and there are not many wooded areas that are near it."

After each gave some thought to what Mot had said, they came to a conclusion that if there was an ambush set up for the bandits it would have to be some distance from Ap Bac. This meant that with only about a half day or so walk to Ap Bac they must be very alert and plan well. They were concerned if there would be spies along the trail to inform someone of their progress and an ambush could be set up in any tree line before you got there. The main question they asked themselves was whether or not they could avoid the trail and wooded areas.

Mot stated that, "Working as a guide for various groups there were many times I needed to avoid some areas so I made my own trails bypassing unwanted areas. That's the same thing Invisible One did when he moved around the back of wooded areas to scout. I am a guide, after all, and I think I can find our way from here bypassing the Son Binh village completely. We would leave out the backside of here and go across country making our own trail. It could mean a little longer trip, but we would be safer. One drawback would be to not resupply ourselves in its market place."

"I pretty much agree with what Mot says," Van Ba told the Invisible One. There is another point to be made also. If we are being watched it would be by people who are familiar with this area and we must consider that they already know we are here and would know when we leave. Eventually they would check out these woods and find we were gone. They would be stumped as to where we are located for a while. Eventually though, our trail would be found and we probably would be tracked and hunted down like animals."

"We need to get out of here much earlier than normal, then. Maybe we should leave when the moon is at its height. That means we only get a little sleep. Once we're on the move every now and then I can drop back and hide to see if we are being followed and if so, try to do something about it. Mot, you've come up with another good idea. The one thing more we must consider is whoever is watching will let the enemy know which way we went. If they pick up our trail they will have some means to communicate with each other and inform the enemy. That means there will be several of them. We will still have to be alert for watchers and an ambush," The Invisible One offered.

Mot added, "Maybe there will be ways we can wipe out a part of our trail at times. That would confuse any follower for a short while and give us a little more time. We might even be able to change directions at times to throw them off balance. We can use streams and small paths to create false trails. We must be careful though in patches of tall grass. It's much harder to hide your trail in broken grass and weeds."

"That may be possible Mot. There may not be too many places for watchers to hide," Van Ba mused. "I don't know if they could get ahead of us and hide in a wooded area to spy, but just in case we need to be careful nearing any wooded area."

They made their plans for standing guard that night and making an early morning departure. Mot would take the first watch, Van Ba the second watch, and the Invisible One the last. Each one would have about four hours to sleep. It was decided not to take time to eat before they left and they would move as quickly as possible. The two guys went to sleep and Mot, standing first watch, wondered around their site on guard, silently and watchful, listening to all of the night noises and being alert for any sounds that were different.

Nothing unusual happened during the short night and they loaded up, moved to the far back corner of the woods slowly and as quietly as possible. When there, Mot checked the moon's position and decided their direction of travel. She pointed in one direction and whispered, "Ok guys, let's go!" They started out at a pace just short of a run. Their bodies were reacting to their lack of sleep and rest, but they continued on for a couple of hours.

They finally ducked into a thicket to take a short rest and eat some bread and drink. They were becoming physically spent. However, they were determined to continue as quickly as possible. After a short rest they started out again at a slightly slower pace and after a while slowed even more.

The moon was much lower in the sky and they could see a slight bit of daylight in the east. They felt the need to hide somewhere to eat and rest before they collapsed. They firmly believed it would be only a couple hours or so before they were missed. Right now, they were ahead of the game and could afford to take the time for a break.

A half hour later they entered a nice-looking thicket, made an impromptu camp, ate dried fish and had a short nap. Mot cut a small limb from a tree that had a lot of leaves on it to brush out their tracks in some areas. Moving out of the thicket they felt groggy and their legs ached from their lack of sleep and rest and the burden they carried. Figuring they were well ahead of any potential watchers they plodded on at their normal pace, still placing one aching leg and foot in front of the other, sometimes winching at the pain.

Mot was true to her word. They created false trails in streams and used the tree limb to obliterate their trail on dusty paths while changing directions. This made the trek even longer and more exhausting. A small clearing about a quarter of a mile off the trail they were cutting offered them a resting place midmorning.

Once comfortable, Mot explained to them, "I believe over there a few miles to the east, is Son Binh Village Headquarters. A little south west of it will be Ap Bac Hamlet. When we leave here we must move west for a while before trying to move south east to find the main trail. I can tell you right now from my experience we need to rest for a day. The pace we started out with really sapped our energy and even a half rest if you two agree. Even then we don't know how safe we'll be here or if it will give our enemies a chance to get ahead of us. Our bodies really need two-or three-day's resting, but time wise we'll have to settle for maybe, one day."

The two tired and achy men gave this idea a lot of thought before either one answered Mot. The Invisible One spoke up first. "I guess it's damned if we do and damned if we don't. We could be screwed either way. Fallout from fatigue or get caught. If we stay here now and leave at first light or a little later how much longer do you think it will take us to find the main trail Mot?"

"Let me see." She thought for a moment. "First we move west for maybe three or four hours and then by angling south east to the main trail rather than straight south it could be another day and a half's journey or more depending on how we take evasive steps to protect ourselves. We could get lucky of course. There may be a small hamlet or two of them along the way where we can replenish or food supplies. We are running low on food. We also could use some better shoes. Ours are getting pretty worn. Our trip has really been hard on them and on our feet too."

Van Ba saw they were looking at him waiting for a comment. After giving some thought he noted, "I think you're both right. We don't know which way is the safest to go and we really do need more supplies. I think we should we stay here for now. We might be able to get a fire going that's almost smokeless and cook what's left of our wilting vegetables, some rice and hot tea now and then rest. There should be enough leftovers for the morning meal. We really need the nourishment and the rest. If we should run into trouble up the road we'll need as much energy as possible. Might I suggest we wait and make the decision on leaving here and how much to eat in the morning before leaving when we're rested more?"

His companions agreed with him and he started gathering twigs and small limbs for the fire while the others moved a little farther in to the clearing and began making their camp site. After the fire was built Mot soon had everything cooking and the aroma was fantastic. While the vegetables and rice cooked they sat on their mats and slowly drank their hot tea and felt the calmness and the serenity in their present setting.

After eating the fire was put out and they lay stretched out on their mats and covers and in a blink of an eye they were sound asleep. Mot awoke just before dusk, got up and looked around. The guys were still asleep and wouldn't miss her for several minutes. She took a small limb with some small branches with lots of green leaves on it to where they had entered and brushed their trail leading to their site, as clean as she could, then she went to her man's mat and laid her warm and tender, yet achy body against Van Ba and even in his sleep he put an arm around her and pulled her close and she went straight to dream land with him.

The Invisible one woke a little after midnight and admired the sleeping pair. While looking at Van Ba and Mot lying next to each other, holding on for dear life, he reminisced. He kind of wished sometimes he could have a beautiful wife to go home to after a mission, but his dedication to the No Name took all of his time. He searched the clearing and around their site and finding nothing unusual he laid his body back onto the mat to sleep.

A little later Van Ba awoke and moved away from the camp site, farther than the Invisible One had scouted earlier, just to relieve his bladder. just before he began to relieve himself he heard a strange noise coming from the other side of the copse. Putting his other brain, that's what Mot called it, back in his pants, he took out his knife and searched the copse silently. He could see some guy sitting on a mat seeming to be half asleep. He snuck back and woke up the other two. He told them that some guy was camping out in the copse also. It was a really odd coincidence to them. Who could be there with them that time of the day, except an enemy?

Leaving Mot at their site the two men split up and stealthily snuck up on the intruder and jumped him from two sides. He was around seventeen years old, fairly strong, was scared out of his wits, nearly crapped in his pants and did soak the front of his pants when the two men suddenly jumped out of nowhere and apprehended him. He knew he was a dead man for sure. The fear of the unknown was making his stomach churn. Grasping his arms, the two guys pulled him to their camp site and set him down hard on one of the mats. Mot, in a very stern manner stared at him, pulled out her knife and asked the guys, "Can I cut them off now?"

Responding to her question the Invisible One said, "At least wait until we've questioned him. His balls will still be there when we're done with him. There wasn't much left of the other guy to talk about anything the last time you castrated a man. It was pretty gory too. There was so much blood. It really spurted everywhere when you cut the guy's throat.

"I can't wait too long. I've had no excitement in the last few days," Mot retorted while staring at the guy with unblinking eyes. The guy quivered a bit. She continued to hone the knife she had taken out when they entered with the kid.

"Ok, I get you! When I'm done with the questions and have some answers you get to do your thing. This time do it so the blood spurts away from us. Van Ba and I had to get different clothes because ours were so bloodied up," the Invisible One commented.

Van Ba had gone back to get the man's gear, stopped to relieve himself first, and now returned to their site with it. He addressed the young man while searching through it saying," Don't worry turd. We'll split your gear between us. We'll take good care of it. You won't need it anymore when we're done with you." At this the young man was really scared half out of his wits. He looked at his captors with pleading eyes and started sobbing and pleading with them.

He never expected to be kidnapped by a bunch of crazy people. That woman, as beautiful as she is, looks really fierce. He hoped that if he kept acting like a cowardly jerk they may take pity on him.

"Let me set you straight. First for our records we need you to give us your real name, what you're doing here in this copse with us, and where your asshole friends are right now. I don't expect any derogatory remarks or lies from you either. You've got three Items that can be carved off at a minutes notice. The third item is your head. You can reason out what the first two are. That woman is more than ready to do it! Each time you lie we'll pull your pants down a little at a time until you are naked. Then it will be her turn at you. Now answer the first two questions!"

"Who are you?"

"What are you doing in the backside of this wooded area?"

CHAPTER 9

AFTER THE YOUNG MAN had been grabbed by Van Ba and the Invisible One they needed to find out why the young man was where he was, and what did he know. "Hey kid, I said, what is your name numb skull?" The Invisible One demanded of the kid, seeming impatient.

Trembling and looking at each of the trio one at a time, he finally answered, "Mt name is Trieu Da."

"Do you mean that you are the Great Trieu Da who united Southern China and Northern Viet Nam down through the Red River delta as far as Da Nang and called it Nam Viet?"

"What's that?" the kid answered.

The Invisible One shook his head saying, "Never mind, I didn't expect you to know. Now tell me Da, and you need to be truthful about this, what are you doing in this wooded area at this time tonight? And don't lie to me or else!"

"Still unsure of his situation and keeping up his act he kind of stuttered and said, "I was told to be here until day break."

"Very good, who told you to be here?"

"Xinhua"

"Just who is Xinhua?"

"He's a Chinese Mandarin and he forced me to be here."

Van Ba interrupted and spoke to the kid softly and kindly, "I think you need to take a deep breath, relax and tell us your story straight from the beginning, young man. If you are sincere and truthful to us no harm will come to you, but if you're not I can't vouch for what my friends might do to you. Especially Mot and her sharp knife! She's an expert with it. I will give you a couple of minutes to consider the offer, so think hard. After a couple of minutes, the offer will be off the table so to speak." He felt the kid would fall for the Bad Guy, Good Guy approach technique. He did.

It only took the kid less than a minute to answer. "What do you want to know?"

The Invisible One turned and walked a few steps over to Mot, with a smile on his face the kid couldn't see, and let Van Ba continue the interrogation while she and he observed.

"Start with where you live and then how you come to know this Xinhua, and what he wanted you to do."

"I live in Quang Tin Hamlet #2. Two days ago, I was riding my water buffalo back to my hovel from the field and I was stopped by this Mandarin. He wanted to know if I was part Chinese and I told him yes, I think I am. He bade me to dismount and follow him into the sub-hamlet. Since he looked very important to me, I did as I was told. He led me to a hovel at the far end of my sub hamlet and told me to enter. I asked why and he said that was unimportant and that unworthy people do not question his authority. So, I entered without any more questions as he had ordered me to do."

"There were six other men there. I don't know if any of them were part Chinese or not. They all looked very mean. I was told to sit and I did. I was afraid not to. The Mandarin gave me his name, Xinhua, and that the ugliest guy was Nguyen Phat, the second in command. He informed me that he had asked people all around the sub-hamlet in regards to who knew the area well, would be the best guide for someone and was told that it would be me. Then he said, "You work for me now and you will do as I command you or else you will never ride your buffalo again. I believed he meant I would be killed if I didn't obey him."

He continued, "One of the men gave me a bag of supplies and we left the hovel. We walked a little till we found a certain trail and stopped. Xinhua asked me about the trails from Tra Ke #4 and if there were any way to leave the main trails and travel around Son Binh village and Ap Bac Hamlet. I let him know that there were no trails or paths, but if you knew the area any at all you could cut your own trail and move around the Village and no one would know the difference. He wanted to know if there were any wooded areas along that way where persons could camp or hide. I told him that there was flat land for a long way from where we were and there would be some wooded areas too. So, he had me guide them to here."

Van Ba asked, "You mean they are here in this wooded area?"

"No! Not this one. They are in the next wooded area down there. He pointed in the direction. I was told to come to this one, search it, to report back if anyone was in it, and if not to watch from where you found me and keep my eyes open for a man and a woman coming this way. If I saw them, I was to go to him right away and let him know. When you two jumped me, I was sitting there wondering how I'd get out of this mess I'm in. I fear I would be killed once the Mandarin got what he wanted and no longer needed me."

"Tell me young man! Are they all in one spot there?" Mot asked.

The kid looked at her and said, "I don't talk to women or answer their questions!"

Van BA grabbed Da's tunic by the collar with both hands, shook him violently, and said, "You do to this woman. Don't forget, she has the knife and I can guarantee you that she will not hesitate to use it on any man. Even me. I wouldn't dare to cross her either. She wouldn't hesitate to castrate me in a heartbeat while I slept." Then he removed his hands after shoving the kid back.

Gulping, the kid mumbled, "Forgive me woman! No, I won't forget again! I'll answer your questions. Five of them are in a clearing close to the middle of it and one at each side of the grove to watch for the pair they seek."

"So, then the watchers are at the far ends and that there's no one between us and the next wooded area?"

"Yes, I guess so."

"Do you know the names of any of the others?" queried The Invisible One.

"Well, Nguyen Phat seemed to be the Number Two man and a Trich Tuy seemed to be Number Three. I don't know any of the others names. It was always those two receiving and giving out the Mandarin's orders. I never did hear the other men's names mentioned even when they spoke to one another. I did hear a couple of the gang say something about some guys they were to meet along the trail with a package never arrived and that they were really concerned about it. Otherwise I never heard anything else the guys discussed that caught my attention. Only cursing about the ones that didn't contact them."

"You're doing great!" Van Ba told him. "Stay relaxed young man. Do they have any kind of weapons with them? If so, what kind of weapons do they have and what knowhow and training to use them?"

"The Mandarin doesn't have any. I think he's a pansy. He is haughty and he seems namby pamby and kind of womanish if that means anything. The others have long knives, but I don't know if they know how to use them or know how to fight."

"Do you know what do they plan to do to the man and the woman after they get the package?"

"I heard them, the top three talking about the man and woman when they told me to come here. I think they want to get a special package that they carry, then to kill them." He looked at Mot and said, "I'm sorry to say this lady, but if you're the beautiful woman they're looking for, and you are very beautiful, they talked about using you by all the gang several times over before the doing the killing. I also heard something about making the guy watch them do it, and they might even do him too before his death."

"Those cockroaches," Mot replied angrily, "don't know who they're fucking with kid. They are dead meat, mark my words. Maybe I'll use their neck bones to sharpen my knife after I castrate them!"

"Easy my dear," Van Ba replied to her. Just do all but one. We need the Mandarin alive with or without his balls."

"The kid was now thinking that these were not bandits as he had thought and for some unknown reason told them, "I believe you are not bad people and I think you should go back the way you came. There are seven of them and only three of you. I'll tell them I never saw you. To begin with, I didn't want to be here at all and I don't want to see any one die, especially me. I just want to plow and ride my buffalo. If I would have known this was going to happen, I would have run from the Mandarin when he first approached me."

Van Ba, after thinking a bit, speaking softly once more tried to reassure him, "It'll be all right for you son. We'll make sure you'll get back to your buffalo and farm your fields soon enough, young man. Did you notice if these guys were really tired, hungry, and sore from their recent travels?"

"I did hear some complaints about them not having much rest or the opportunity to eat their fill the last couple of days. When the Mandarin would hear them carp, he'd look at Nguyen Phat and Phat would tell them to shut up and keep moving or they would suffer the consequences."

"Do any of them have any physical problems you know of?"

"I think they all have sore legs and feet, and maybe a couple of them have sore backs from the extra load they carried for the Mandarin. One guy did limp a little bit; but he'd turned his ankle on a rock."

"Did you hear Xinhua say why he wanted the package?"

The kid was starting to lose his fears and was now much calmer, and after giving it some thought, stated, "No he didn't say anything at all about the package, but he kept on cursing some secret society, something about it having no name or something like that, and saying to Phat that he would destroy it completely one way or another."

"Ok, I have one more question for you and it's very important. Did you hear them speak of any more gangs up ahead waiting for us?"

"I think I heard Xinhua telling Nguyen Phat and Trich Tuy that this would be the groups last chance for them to get the Package and anyone who dared to fail to do so or screws it up dies."

Van Ba spoke earnestly to the young man. "I cannot but laud and thank you for being so open and honest with us. I think you'll grow up to be an honest and trustworthy man. Maybe even a great one. Those guys wo took you away from your land and buffalo are the bad ones and they would bring down our country if left unchallenged by ones like us. They are a danger to every man and woman in Nam Viet. You've done the right thing by cooperating and being honest with us. We applaud you." Van Ba didn't want him to feel bad about giving out information on the gang.

The Invisible One placed a hand on Da's shoulder and spoke softly and friendly to him. "Please Da, don't worry about the three of us against seven. We are with the No Name society, these two are top notch martial artists and I am the Invisible One. I'm sure you heard of me many times."

"You don't expect me to believe that do you? I've heard the Invisible One is never seen or heard until he strikes."

"That's right, but it's only when invisibility is needed to catch scumbags like the scum that forced you to come with them."

"Hearing about your exploits I always wanted to be like you and if not, maybe I could work the rice paddies and along the Red River where our goods come in and till our junks come home. Then I could get a get a bride and elope on one and work every day to be as smart, strong, and agile as you are. Maybe train the wife too, and then we could have adventures together."

"You have a good dream so keep working hard toward it young Da. It will come true for you some day. And I do hope it comes true for you. You seem like a very nice young man. Now, we three must make our plans. We will move over there so as not to bother you. While we are over there you rest easy here and think hard about anything else you can tell us. We will not be long."

The three partners moved about ten feet away. "We need to take them while they asleep if possible. Waking they will be a little groggy and they won't move very easily. I do have a plan in mind," the Invisible One stated. "Tell us, I'm dying to know." Mot replied.

"My first thoughts are of Nguyen Phat and Trich Tuy and the need to eliminate them first, then capturing and getting information from the Mandarin, Xinhua for Nguyen Hai to act on. So, here is my plan."

"Van Ba and I will slip up on the lookouts, each of us taking one guy, and kill him. Then we'll move to their camp and attack them from two sides. Mot, keep an eye on the

Mandarin. He will try to move away to hide or escape. That's your job to keep him there. I have extra knives in the pack I have so Van Ba and I each will fight with two blades and each of us with two men. Is this ok with you two? We can change it if either of you have a better plan. Van Ba and Mot nodded in agreement with him."

"There is one more thing for us to consider. Do either of you feel that this kid is on the level and may want a little payback?" The pair felt that the kid was ok and should be given a chance at payback, whatever that was.

They moved over to the prisoner. The Invisible One told him he had two choices and he must choose quickly. "Da You have two choices. Your first choice is to remain here tied up till we return, if we do return, or second, we release your bonds and you help Mot take down and bind the Mandarin, Xinhua."

"Release me and I will help! I'm mad at being taken from my home like they did. Beautiful lady, tell me what you desire me to do to help and you shall have it." The kid was freed and the Invisible One gave the kid a knife and Mot handed him some rope. Mot motioned to him to follow her a few steps away from the men.

"Have you ever tried to move quietly across land or between trees? If not, I will show you how and you will follow me. We will go slowly. Remember we must go silently and be in position to rush the Mandarin when the two men attack. They will make a lot of noise initially to scare the opponents so don't let it scare you. We may have to chase our man, but we'll catch him. I'll make the threats to him while you tie him up. Do his knees first, that way we can make him walk slow steps when we want to move him. He sure won't run from us then. Then bind his hands behind his back. Then I will put a loop around his neck, making a leash. That's what we will control him with. He'll feel somewhat degraded so every once in a while, tell him how lowly he is, how worthless, and other things you might think up. I will leave you with the Mandarin and go to help the men fight and you bring him along so he can see the last of his men while they're still alive."

"I'll do my best for you lady. I think I've changed my mind about you three. I've never been around anyone who seemed so confident in what they do. Maybe we will win. I think I'm going to like this. It's making me feel more alive already."

Van Ba and the Invisible One stepped over to Mot and Da. The Invisible One looked at and said to Da, "Da, walk with me to the woods edge over there. These love birds need to talk between them a little before we leave here. They'll come along soon, so come with me." They walked away.

"Mot, my dearest Woman," Van Ba said pulling her close, "This time together could be the last for either or both of us. You're so beautiful and I love you so much. Your young body has given me the vigor of youth I never thought I'd ever experience again. I'm sorry we weren't able to make love the last couple nights, and have no chance for our last time here. Always remember I want to marry you and have as many children with you as you want to have with me." He kissed her hard.

"Oh Van Ba," she said with a tear in her eyes, I feel the same way to. I want to marry you and have many babies by you. I also want to learn from my teacher all those other things you want to teach me, especially the one where you give me something to eat, I think you said. Oh shit, we better go before I really start crying." They pulled each other even closer and had one more, deep, and loving kiss. Then, holding each-others hands, they went to meet the others. She dried her eyes with her shirt sleeve.

The invisible one looked at each one and gave a little pep talk. "This could be the last hurtle we must face. I sure hope so. We are getting very tired and worn down. If we find out from Xinhua that there are no more hazards we can rest and finish our journey in a pleasant way while enjoying each other's company. Just think what it would be like if we were to deliver Xinhua along with the package to Nguyen Hai. Let's stand in a circle, put our right hand on the left shoulder of the one to your right and swear to our solidarity this night and to the security of our country." They did.

"Da, you and Mot wait here about twenty minutes. That will give us time to sneak up and take out the guards then work your way as close as you can to the Mandarin. When you hear us screaming to high heaven and attacking the thugs go for him." He and Van Ba stole silently towards the next wooded area and their fate.

While they were waiting for the guys to enter the next wooded area, Mot smiled, looked at the kid and spoke kindly to him, "Since we're both in this together I think you should call me Mot. I hate being called lady or woman, and only Van Ba calls me woman. That's because I am his Woman. Is that going to be all right with you, Da?"

"Oh my! Yes, it is! Mot, I only called you lady because I didn't know what else to say to you. I've always had trouble talking with beautiful women, but I think I'll be all right talking with you now."

"That's ok Da. You'll find that I'm very easy to talk with. Van Ba is also easy to talk with even though he seems gruff at times. The men have entered the woods so let us begin our part." Mot moved bent over from the waist and moved quietly and slowly across the open area between the woods. Da followed imitating her every move.

When they entered the woods, Mot stopped him and using her hands as indicators, showed Da how to step quietly and to hold branches to keep them from snapping back and causing an unwanted noise. Then she motioned him to follow her and they moved deeper into the trees until they approached the clearing and saw their enemies. They were lucky, the group was asleep and the Mandarin was sleeping closest to them, slightly apart from the others. They waited quietly and patiently for the attack to begin, as they could.

Meanwhile, Van Ba and the Invisible One both accomplished what they set out to do. Both of the sentries were sitting up and half asleep very close to the edge of the woods where they could observe the clear areas. The duo crept up on their individual targets and took them out using the same method. They jammed a knee onto the prey's back, at the same time reaching around grabbing the mouth, nose and chin, tilting the head back and slicing their blade across the neck, avoiding the blood spray as much as possible and letting the victim fall over. Each one rummaged through the prey's gear, found nothing useful, then they began to move towards the clearing, silently and deadly. They had agreed to give each other time enough to take out the guards and converge on opposite sides of the clearing. By pre-arrangement Van Ba would wait, since he was the nearest one to them, until his comrade screamed and started towards the group, then to confuse them Van Ba would scream and start his attack from the other side; Mot and Da would then go for the Mandarin.

Mot, and especially Da, was getting a little impatient after a while, hoping that nothing had happened to the men. Then suddenly all hell broke loose. After closing on the camp, the Invisible One suddenly charged the clearing screaming at the top of his lungs from one side and Van Ba came screaming from the other, both swinging two knives in circular movements. The sleeping men scared out of their somnambulistic states jumped up, trying to get awake, find their orientation and bearings and were grabbing for their knives.

The Mandarin also jumped up fearing for his life and turned to run and ran smack into Mot and Da. The two grabbed him and pulled him into the trees throwing him down on his face. Mot put her knee in his back, the dull side of her knife against his throat and told him his useless ass was dead if he moved a muscle. Da quickly bound his knees together then pulled his hands behind his back and tied them very tight. Xinhua tried to complain, but Mot tied a strip of cloth around his mouth and told him to shut up or she would cut his lying ass tongue out. The two sat him up and Mot took the long rope that was coiled around her waist, made a noose and quickly placed it over his neck, tightening it only to the point where he could still breathe. The Mandarin had never been so scared in his unworthy life. The Mandarin had never been in such a predicament like this. The shoe had always been on the other guy's foot.

Da slapped Xinhua hard across the face a couple of times for good measure, spat at him, and told him, "You dirty filthy bastard, now it's my turn to be the big shit. You hear me? You're going to find out just how lowly and useless you really are. You are below a water buffalo's dung heap. You will pay for forcing me to follow you and to do your bidding, you cockroach pig, you! You'll never crawl out from under this dung heap."

Then he kicked the Mandarin in the ribs causing Xinhua to try to scream through the gag. Mot watching this smiled. Watching him she realized that Da was a quick learner and was glad he joined them on this escapade. She handed the end of the rope to Da. "Don't pull too hard on the leash. We need him alive, at least until after the interrogation is over."

The Mandarin hearing this wet his pants, although it couldn't be seen because of his long robe, but could be smelt. He was scared shitless. "You keep him entertained here. I've got to go help Van Ba and the Invisible One," and she took off towards the melee pulling her knife out as she ran.

Da could now smell the Mandarin's fluid. Look at you, you stinking pig. You smell worse than the most useless swine or its dung heap.

When she took off to help Van Ba, Da was getting very impatient and wanted to join the melee. So, he tied the Mandarin to a tree while making as many derogatory remarks to him as he possibly could, told him they'd bring his mother to him to have sex with, slapped him a few more times across the face, kicked him in the groin then followed after Mot, determined to help her and the guys any way he could.

The Invisible One was enjoying himself. He was parrying the thrusts and jabs from the two he believed were Nguyen Phat and Trich Tuy using martial art movements named after animals. Being younger, more nimble and spryer than the two older ones was right up his alley. As he darted between and around them time after time he would cut them lightly on the arms, thighs or sides. Both dudes cursed him and begged him to quit dancing around like a woman he is and fight like a man. He did once by stopping and bringing the dull edges of both long knives of his down on to the top of both shoulders of Trich Tuy, who fell to the ground where he stood. He turned to dodge a thrust by Nguyen Phat and faked a counter stroke. Trich Tuy stood and grimacing against the pain in his shoulders rejoined the fight, not realizing that he was not long for this world.

After several minutes, the Invisible One decided he was tired of playing around with these two asses and picked Trich Tuy to die first. He lowered one of his long knives, faking a strike at the legs then swung it up in an arch and catching the guy's wrist, nearly cutting off the hand with the knife. He let his blade continue to rise to its peak and slashed it down into the foe's neck almost decapitating the head of his opponent. He watched the man sink slowly to the ground. Then he turned his attention to Nguyen Phat who had paused to take a breath when he saw the way his partner was taken out.

The Invisible One then exclaimed to Phat, "Phat! You've been a determent to our Country, Nguyen Hai, and me, and you've been a pain in the ass to the No Name for too long a time. Now it's time for you to pay your dues to Buda, country, and die like the vile, stinking rodent you really are. I just need to figure out if I should play around with you a little more or just go ahead and whack your fucking head head off, or I could start with cutting your balls off. We've got a lady with us who would just love to do that to you. That might be impossible though. I've been told that you must have balls before they can be cut off."

"You're a young unworthy puke for a man. I don't know who you think you are mister high and mighty, but I'm a better fighter than you any day. You need to pray to Buda or whoever you pray to, if you do pray at all, right now because you're as good as dead. Come to me and meet your ancestors!"

"If it was anyone but you, I wouldn't waste time telling you who I am. However, you are a very special case to me. I am The Invisible One. I am Nguyen Hai's special messenger who sends the scum of the earth to meet with their ancestors time after time. You are about meet yours whether they want you there or they don't. They probably don't want a rodent like you near them at all."

The Invisible One continued on. "Nguyen Hai has commissioned me to do whatever I need to do to rid our people and our country of you and scum bags like you. You have been a spear in the side of the people for too long now. In a moment no one will ever have to fear you again. I have only one last thing I need to say to you before you die by my long knife. Now your ass is grass, you ass."

Hollering, "You Die, you Bastard!" Nguyen Phat suddenly lunged at him, thrusting his long knife straight in front of him to stab with and was side stepped by the Invisible One to his right and gave Phat a light slash across the back. He stumbled in pain, turned to face his foe and was greeted with a long knife into his groin area. Phat sank to his knees grabbing the wound and with a spinning move and with the swipe of his sharp blade the Invisible One took his head off with one long smooth slash.

He looked at the headless corpse prone on the ground, kicked the head, and said to it, "I'm Sorry you had to leave here so soon. Our party is over to soon. Now you are part of the grass, you ass. The rest party is just getting started, but you still lost the grand prize any how."

CHAPTER 10

Van Ba was having a rough time against his two opponents. The two men he was fighting were a lot younger, were stronger, some-what coordinated, and were in good shape. He realized they had had some training too, and most likely somewhat experienced at knife fighting. He was constantly jumping, spinning, slashing, and blocking the thrusts and jabs of his opponents with his two long knives and trying to execute moves of his own. He already had some small cuts on his forearms and biceps which were bleeding along with a shallow slash on his back, one across his chest and on one leg. Van Ba was bloody and tiring and wondered just how soon he'd cease to exist as a man. Try as he might he wasn't able to put either of the two young men down yet to make it a one on one fight.

When Mot exited the trees, she was horrified at the sight of a bloody Van Ba fighting for his life. She then wielded her own knife in his defense, bent over and quietly charged toward towards the melee. The three men were so busy fighting they did not see Mot's movement towards them. She reached the back of one of the two enemies and made a long slashing stroke cutting a deep gash into the back of both the one guy's thighs, his blood spurting out and he immediately fell to his knees screaming. Mot kicked him in the nape of his neck knocking him flat on his face. She straddled his back, grabbed his hair pulling his head back and cut his throat then jumped up to go to Van Ba's defense. She was amazed at what she saw. There was Da faking lunges with his knife, and jumping back and forth at the other guy, and along with his buddy's scream, was distracting him and giving Van Ba an edge. Van Ba was gaining ground and was forcing the man backwards and Da was still doing fakes against him.

The man suddenly decided that the better part of valor was living to fight another day. He pleaded to the man in front of him who refused to fall to allow him to surrender and as he dropped his knife Mot leaped at him with a jump kick and caught him beside his head stunning and knocking him ass over tin cups. She was on him and rolled the guy onto his stomach sat on his back. "Da," she commanded, "Come over here and sit on his back, and place your knife against his throat. If he should so much as takes a breath, moves a muscle, even a little, cut it". The man coming around made sure they knew he'd comply peacefully. Da hopped on his back and placed his knife where he had been directed. Mot looked at him and demanded, "Where in the hell is the Mandarin? Did he get away and how did he do it?"

Smiling at Mot he let her know, "I tied him up to a tree. He's angry as hell, but patiently waiting for us to bow to his every wish, Ha! Ha! Oh, he may have sore balls too along with a sore jaw. I think it keeps him from talking really well."

"Dam if you aren't the smart one. Well, I guess you'll do in a pinch. Thanks for helping Van Ba. I was very proud of the way you acted in distracting this guy." She turned around and what she saw made her heart sink. Van BA had collapsed and was panting heavily trying to catch his breath. His several wounds, although not real serious by themselves, were still bleeding a lot. He was exhausted, his eyes were closed, his breathing was shallow and he was looking like death warmed over. She rushed to him with tears flowing from her eyes and calling his name. She dove to her knees beside of him and took his head in her arms. She kept saying, "Don't die! Don't die! Don't leave me! I need you! She kept hugging him tightly and weeping."

"His breathing was momentarily a little better, but was very fatigued from the exertion of his journey, the fight and the loss of blood from his wounds. He opened his eyes and muttered in a low tone, "I'm not going any place woman, not very soon any way. Know your place woman and kiss me passionately." She did, long and deep. Then she started checking his wounds, seeing they were not real deep, nonlife threatening or real debilitating, grabbed one of the blankets lying on the ground and cut it in strips, went back to her man and without removing his bloody clothes, began to bandage his wounds, binding them tightly to help stem the blood flow.

The Invisible One had finally finished the game of playing with his foes. Now that his bout was over, he thought of Van Ba and turned to go to his aid and was relieved to see Mot bandaging him up. Then he spotted Da sitting on a man's back with his knife to his throat and laughed, re-leaving a built-up stress. He thought, "This kid does have promise after all." He rummaged through a couple of the group's bags and found some rope, cut a couple of lengths and went over and bound their prisoner. Then he moved to Mot and Van Ba's side to see if he could help her care for her nearly fallen hero.

Mot said to the Invisible one. "We need to get him comfortable and resting. He is just out of it from all that stress and strain we've been under for days, the fight and a loss of blood. We can clean his wounds and change his bandages later when the bleeding stops. She and the Invisible One gathered the sleeping mats and blankets from the fallen ones. She put three mats on top of each other and they very carefully moved Van Ba to the mats and laid him down and she used two blankets to cover him.

The Invisible One opined that, "Mot, I think you must stay here and care for your man while Da and I will move along and cover up the bodies somewhere away from this clearing and then round up ours and the guard's loads and we'll set up here for a day or two. Did you see, by any chance, which direction the Mandarin escaped to? I need to catch that ass and bring him to Nguyen Hai."

"He didn't escape Invisible One. Da and I caught him and bound him, and when I went to help Van Ba in his fight, Da tied him to a tree and came to help us out. I'll tell you all about it later. I'm proud of him!"

"That's very good Mot! You too Da! You two did great! We'll tie this other one to a tree also. We'll move the Mandarin to another tree too. We need to keep a good watch over them at all times. It wouldn't be good for us for either of them to get loose and go for help or whatever. It's almost day light out now so I think I'll restart their fire which is now our fire. Thanks to our enemies there are already some twigs, limbs, and branches piled up here. When I get it going, we'll pull your guy closer to it to help keep him warm and comfortable. We can question the two prisoners later. We'll just let them suffer and wonder what their fate will be and when we'll get to it."

He got the fire restarted, helped move Van Ba close to it then he and Da tied the two prisoners securely to separate trees where they could be watched. He walked over and smiled at her and said, "When Van Ba goes to sleep you need to sleep too. I know you'll want to take care of him but you will need your rest also to be able to do so. There is one more thing I need to say, and you can tell your husband to be, I'm very happy to have met you two. I could not have asked for nicer, stronger, more determined and faithful people to have on a mission with me. You two are the greatest team mates I've ever worked with. Nguyen Hai will be as proud of you two as I am." With that he motioned to Da and they were on their way to take care of the bodies and collect the gear.

When the two left, she put down another mat beside Van Ba, stepped over to grab a blanket and she heard a terrible sound. She spun around and realized what it was. Van Ba was snoring like a wild animal growling at the world. She smiled at her man and lay beside him and pulled the cover over her and laid an arm over her lover and was so happy he wasn't hurt worse, or yet, gone to his ancestors. She had never before felt the way she does about him or any other man she'd ever come in contact with. It wasn't long before she was in dream land too, making mad passionate love with Van Ba.

The sun was high in the sky and they were awakened by the Mandarin trying to shout for food and water and respect for his station. Somehow the gag Mot had put around his mouth had slipped down. Da stood up and took his water bladder over and gave him a drink, then gave one to the other prisoner. He walked back to his mat and went back to sleep. The Invisible one threw more kindling on the fire, Mot got out the tea and cooking pots, rummaged through various bags and began to prepare a meal. Van Ba seemed to be sleeping peacefully, breathing more normal, and thank goodness, not snoring any more.

She was glad the Mandarin's screeching didn't wake him. When the food was ready, she would feed him then they would remove his clothes, clean and re-bandage the wounds. While doing this she would have Da dig out any extra clothes from the enemy's bags for him. Then she would try to get him to go back to sleep. They would stay where they were for the night resting up. In the morning they would decide when to leave depending on Van Ba's condition. If need be, they could spend an additional night and a day for Van Ba to recover more. Mot would take care of her man, but she wanted him to be as strong as possible before they moved on. Of course, when they did leave, she would split Van Ba's load between the guys. The guys wouldn't care a bit, they were still young and strong. Right now, though, there was a great need for staying in this clearing a couple of days and letting Van Ba recover his health and letting his wounds heal as much as possible.

When the meal of rice, vegetables, dried fish, bread and tea was ready, she called the other two to get their food then moved to Van Ba. She sat beside him and gently shook his shoulder. He had a very hard time waking up. After the arduous journey, the fatiguing fight, the wounds and blood loss from last night's fight he was physically exhausted and needed to regain his strength. His eyes were finally opening a little at a time, and Mot cooed to him, "Hey you! Old man! Are you with us to day or not? I hope so. You need to wake up and let your mama feed you some food. The other stuff later."

Starting to get fully awake the pain in his limbs from the fight, and his and wounds sent shockwaves surging through his body. "Oh Buda! Damn I hurt!" he muttered. "What has happened to me?" Then he began to remember. "I didn't do very good in the fight last night, did I Mot."

"Before I tell you how much a brave and fierce a warrior you were last night, and how proud of you I am of my hero, it must have knocked some good sense into you. You called me Mot instead of Woman. I like the sound of it even though I was getting used to being called, Woman, by you. Please Van Ba! Call me Mot more often! I really like the sound of it when you speak my name."

"Well ok Woman, if you insist, Mot." She gave him a playful slap on the face. "Mot! I was stupid for taking on those two young guys by myself. I'm not as young and agile as I once was. I was in over my head, but I was sure glad to see young Da pretending to fight with that knife to distract the guy and the way you took down that other guy. I didn't think he had it in him. He's not the little coward he pretended to be. I had faith in you and you didn't let me down. I had doubted I would even finish the fight alive and your' and his actions gave me the strength to end it. I did end it, didn't I?"

"I'll be truthful! He surrendered to us when he saw he was alone against three of us. Turn you head and look over there. See the two asses tied to the trees. That's what we accomplished because of your superb fighting. Not many guys could have held out like you did. It gave us the time to complete our task and come to help." Van Ba finally was able to sit part way up and lean close to Mot. She got teary, put her lips close to his ears and whispered, "I was so afraid for you and I almost collapsed when I saw you bleeding and fighting for your life. I never killed a man before like I did last night. After the other one surrendered, I turned around and saw you laying there on the ground and I was so afraid you were dead. I need to talk to you about it to ease my mind when this is over and we're finally alone. I was happy I did it to save you, but it was horrible for me at the same time."

"Don't fret my love. When you're ready we'll have a nice talk. I know you're hurt from the killing, but I am so proud of you for the act. You saved my life. I'm so glad you did.

Damn! I Guess I'm stuck with you for life now. Now we need only to think about the wonderful family we'll have together. I can hardly wait to give you one hundred-kids, all mean little boys pulling at your legs and getting in your path every minute of the day. In my mind I can see you swatting them out of the way."

"Thank you, Van Ba! I needed to hear you say that. I think you should think about a couple of nice little girls too. They like to help mommy around the hovel, learn to cook, clean, and sew. Now! I'm going to feed you. Not what you want though. When you are done eating, we're going to take off your bandages and clothes and burn them and the bloody mat underneath you. I'll clean your wounds and re-bandage them. Da found some clothes you can wear in the dead guys gear. Then you will go back to sleep and rest some more to help your wounds heal. Understand big boy?"

"I guess." Still winching with pain and exhaustion he managed, "We're not even married yet and I'm already hen pecked to death. Of course, I can't think of a nicer hen to peck me. You're beautiful. Mot, before you burn my clothes you must take everything from inside my tunic. The stuff inside it is important, even if it got a little bloody. I need most of all, Mr. Hu's note to me and the letter for Nguyen Hai. My letter has more instructions to follow to meet Nguyen Hai. We can't lose them."

"Ok. I'll do that for you. Right now, I want you to lie back down and close your eyes and rest while I dish up some food for you and then put on a pot of water to heat so I can cleanse your wounds and clean the blood from the rest of your body."

She put a pot of water on the fire and was dishing up Van Ba's food when she got a thought about water. She called Da over and asked, "Da, we're running low on water. Do you know where there is any stream close by here?"

"I already discussed that with the Invisible One. I know several places between here and the Red River where there is always fresh and cool water and also where we can get the supplies we need for your travel. We won't have to go very far."

"Thank you! Will you help me carry the dishes over to Van Ba? Thanks! Listen, after I feed him, I need you to help me get those awful bloody clothes off of him and then I'll need you to help me dress him after I tend his wounds."

Bowing from the waist to her he responded, "Yes! Yes! And yes! Your Royal Highness, Mot. Your every wish is my command. Just speak and it shall be done!" Grinning Mot slapped him playfully and informed him she was glad he was with them. While they had time on their hands waiting for her guy to recover some, she would have to show him some fighting moves to practice. Even though she was only a couple of years older than him she was surprised how on one hand he was remarkable and how naïve he was on the other hand. She felt she owed him a little education.

She wouldn't let Van Ba feed himself. She insisted that she feed him and as much as he hurt, he enjoyed her wanting to care for him. It was really a new and wonderful experience to have the love of his life care about him. She did most of the talking because she purposely kept his mouth full of food, sometimes too much. She was getting a kick out of it. Finally, he was done eating and she took the dishes away and got the pot of hot water and some rags she'd made and placed them beside him. She needed to let the water cool some so she walked over to Da, took him by the elbow and marched him over to Van Ba. They carefully removed the bandages, then they removed his bloodied clothes and she removed everything from inside his tunic. She let Da go back over to whatever he'd been doing.

She very carefully cleansed and re-bandaged the wounds using the last of the old blanket. Her heart really went out to her man. Every little movement her and Da made prepping him he would flinch and moan. His wounds were very painful and it was nearly unbearable when she washed them. When she finished, she called to Da and both men came over to help dress him. Before they did the dressing, she put his items in the tunic. His papers weren't in bad shape because they were on the opposite side of the chest wound. After dressing Van Ba, they made him comfortable on the two mats and covered him with couple of blankets. As much as he was hurting, he went right back to sleep.

The three friends walked a few steps away at Da's urging. He proposed to them that he felt they should stay and rest an extra day for Van Ba's benefit. The other two agreed whole heartedly. That would mean that Van Ba will have two nights to rest up and begin to heal and recuperate as much as possible. It would also be a good rest for them as their bodies could use the rest, too.

The Invisible One asked Da if he would collect their water bladders, and get some fresh water. The water would be needed due to staying there an extra day. Van Ba looked as bad as Dorothy's wicked witch looked like she did when she was melting.

Da said to the three who were now his friends. "You three people are something else! You'll have your fresh water in about twenty minutes or so," and he left with theirs and the foe's bladders at a run.

The Invisible one said to Mot, "Our friends tied to the trees should be about ready to talk. When Da gets back with the water we'll ask some questions. I haven't had time to set up any scenarios for any approach techniques so we'll just take different roles. Our improve interrogations together have worked well so far on this journey. It's amazing how we have worked together harmoniously without having to have planned or trained together. The Mandarin thinks Da is out of his mind, so we'll let Da piss them off first, maybe even instil a little fear. We can pick up the pace when Da gets them really mad.

"Since we'll interrogate the prisoners one at a time, we can set you close to where they can see you clearly. You can sharpen your knives like you did before, maybe even point the knives at them and we'll have Da make threats to them also." Meanwhile, Da had returned with full water bladders from where ever, and was given an update on questioning the prisoners and what his role would be.

Da casually walked over to the younger one and without warning kicked the guy in the privates. Tied to the tree as he was, he couldn't bend over, but he sure screamed with pain and had tears running down his cheeks. "That's for some of the nasty remarks you made to me along the trail. Don't you worry any about my kick in your private parts. You just need to think about all the rest of them to come. Soon you will see the woman sitting over there and sharpening her knives. I understand she loves to cut the balls off of dirty cockroaches like you. She's really good with a knife. Remember what she did to your buddy. You should have seen those guys back up the trail I understand. They were really a bloody mess I hear. They're now eunuchs and not good for any woman. Of course, they might find another man to live with. Maybe you'll like to get a man when your balls are gone." Smiling, Da stomped on the guy's right foot and got another scream from him. Looking and hearing what was happening, the Mandarin began to feel some fear. "I know you two haven't eaten. It's a shame. The lady is a good cook. I don't know if they'll feed you before they!" Da left off the end of his sentence on purpose and walked over to sit by Mot. Let them contemplate their fates.

The Invisible One had been observing Da's act and was pleased with his actions. He stepped to Da and Mot and addressed Da. "That was great. Where did you learn that technique?"

"My grandfather and my father, after him, worked as part of the hamlet security team. I watched them perform many interrogations. I have to be very honest though. I neither said, nor did anything to him I didn't feel or want to do. Right now, I'd like to do more than that to them. They deserve it the way they treated me."

"Da, normally during an interrogation you must hold back your feelings and emotions. Everything you do and say must be controlled by your play acting; however, there are times when your raw emotions can work to your favor, especially when you're inexperienced. Moving slowly into your questioning helps keep yourself under control also. When you finish your questioning always leave them believing you will want to talk to them again or that you'll keep some kind of contact with them. I can see by the way those two reacted you got the right reactions we need. They believed you right off the bat because of what they forced you to do. I'm glad you mentioned food to them. I can use that when I'm ready to question them. I'm going to turn my back and talk with Mai and you walk slow and purposeful to the Mandarin, grin at him, spit on him, and slug him in the jaw as hard as you can and walk back here. Mot will watch his reaction."

Mot and the Invisible one could hear Da spit and slug the Mandarin really hard. The Mandarin hollered and slumped his head over, out like a light. Mot said, "That was a great shot Da. You're going to have them pissed and scared like we want."

"Thanks, Mot! I needed that."

The Invisible One explained his plan to the two. "We wait a while then we'll take the young one over there where the Mandarin can see but not hear what's going on. We'll stake him down spread eagled and then after a little more intimidation I'll ask questions. Of course, you two can also ask things now and then if you think of something important, and help to keep him confused. Everything we are doing with that guy will prey on the Mandarin. He is used to being treated like an elite and spoiled by everyone. If you look at the young one, you'll see he wet his pants when Da harassed him. We don't know if the Mandarin has done it too because of the knee length gown he's wearing, but he sure smells like it, so, I'll bet he did and that he's scared shitless. We'll really have fun messing up his mind. Let's sit by the fire and have a cup of tea. Mot, would you do us the pleasure of serving us?"

"Well kind sir, I would be enormously proud to do so for such an elegant and honored individual." She had put the pot of water almost on the fire to stay hot after cleaning Van Ba's wounds, so all she had to do was pour it over the tea leaves. The Invisible One sat with his right side towards the prisoners. Every once in a while, he'd turn his shoulders towards them, stretch out his arm with the cup of tea as if offering them a drink, smile and turn back to face Mot and Da. He always liked to messing with cockroach's minds.

When tea time was over, he and Da released the young one from the tree and even though the guy struggled with them, managed to stake him down with his limbs spread out. Mot walked over to him and standing beside him put the dull side of her knife between his legs and informed him, "I'm looking forward to the guys getting done with you. Three of us, me, my knife, and your balls are going to meet, greet, and have a good old time. She lifted the blade and swung it down hitting the intended parts with the dull edge. The guy let out a horrifying scream and thrashed around as much as the restraints would allow. Mot looked down at him and laughed, then walked over and began sharpening her knife where he and the Mandarin could see her.

Da looked on as the Invisible One sat crossed legged beside the guy's head and laid his knife on the ground beside him. "I have some questions for you and guess what? You're going to answer them, isn't that right, you, unworthy cock roach?" The guy was trembling with fear and thrashing around trying to free himself to no avail. The Invisible One picked up his knife and slapped the other side of the guy's face with the flat side of the blade. "Lie still and answer my questions, understand?" That got the guy's attention and he quit thrashing about, but was still scared as hell."

"Well answer me?"

A weak mournful yes came out of his mouth. "I'll do anything you ask. I don't want to be hurt or die. I want to live! Please!"

"Ok! This is how it works. I'll ask questions and you answer them as truthfully as you can. If I think you're lying to me I will do something to you. What I don't know yet, but I am sure I can think of something to amuse me. I might even have Da bring me a water bladder. Do you know what it's like to have water poured into your stomach until it distends? The fun then is a downward blow to the stomach with a fist and you become a water spout. It would be fun for me even though I'd get wet. If you do well though, I'll consider feeding you, keeping you alive and turning you over to Nguyen Hai. If you don't that woman over there likes to play a game with a guy's manhood. You may not know this, but she's really pissed off at you for the wounds and fatigue her husband has suffered at your hands." Sometimes little white lies are useful as an interrogation aid as well as the truth. "I'm just going to sit here very quietly for a few minutes and let you decide what your own fate will be. In a few minutes we'll begin."

The Invisible One sat and stared at the guy without changing his expression for several minutes, just watching the prisoner stew in his juices. Patience was a good virtue to have with some prisoners. To let them stew in their own juices was always an advantage in some interrogations of uneducated ones.

Finally, he asked, "It would be nice to know your name. Of course, I could still call you cockroach if you'd like me to."

"Bui Tinh! That's me."

"Well Tinh, you look larger and more solidly built than most of us Vietnamese. Are you of mixed blood?"

"My father was Chinese and my mother was Chinese and Vietnamese."

"You don't have a Chinese name. Do you know why?"

"My mother wanted me to be named after her father who was killed by a mad water buffalo when she was a young girl."

"I take it from the way you answered that you've decided to cooperate with me, is that right?"

"I don't think I have a better choice. I want to live. What will happen if you turn me over to Nguyen Hai? I'll still be killed, wont I?"

"I'm very close to him. If you cooperate, I'll ask of him that you not be harmed. Besides, Nguyen Hai may be able to use your fighting skills. All you need is a little more training and experience. But that remains to be seen as of yet. First thing I need to know is how you come to be with Xinhua."

"I am a wonderer and I was passing by some rice paddies down by the Red River and I stopped to talk to a rice farmer. While we were talking, Xinhua, Nguyen Phat, and Trich Tuy came by. Xinhua Said I looked Chinese. I told him yes, but also part Vietnamese. He wanted to know about me and I told him about being a wonderer and he explained he needed a crew to help him on a mission and if came with him I would be paid well. It sounded good to me so I agreed. He recruited three Vietnamese from the same area and we followed him to some sub-hamlet. There he gave us provisions and told us he must retrieve a valuable package from some gang and that we would be his security while doing so. He also said that failure to get the package was not an option for him. He didn't tell us the whole truth. I found out during our travel that there was some problem and we would be looking for a man and a woman."

"What did your group do then?"

"We walked about a day and a half to the sub-hamlet where Xinhua inquired about getting a guide for us and the kid over there was named as the best around and he was forced to come with us."

"Was the trip hard on you?"

"Yeah it sure was. I, and the other three Vietnamese, had to carry most of the gear. That Mandarin bastard over there, wouldn't allow us to have very much rest till we got here. If we complained he'd have that Nguyen Phat bitch at us. He's an asshole! I got really tired and my muscles ached at every step I took."

"He's not going to bitch at you anymore Tinh. He's living with his ancestors now. He even became part of the grass. You and the Mandarin are the only two left. Before you took on the kid at the sub-hamlet did you hear much conversation between Xinhua and his two henchmen about their mission?"

"I heard bits and pieces as they spoke at different times. The Mandarin was concerned that they must stop a man and a woman to get some important package at all costs. If they did not get it their lives would be forfeit to some leader someplace else."

"Did they ever say what was in the package?"

"No!"

"Did they say why they needed it?"

"They said something about keeping it from unifying some people, some place, some kind of society or other and that it would be of great value to the Chinese to have it. I never really understood all they were saying, I wasn't close to them."

"Did you know you might have to fight?"

"Nothing was ever said about it, but I wasn't worried."

"Why were you not worried?"

"Wondering here and there I learned some martial arts and a little about knife fighting. I only wanted to learn how to do it so I could protect myself from bandits on the trails."

"Do you know what fate they had planned for the man and especially the woman after capturing them?"

"That worried me a lot. I'm not a rapist or a killer. They talked about doing terrible things to them and then killing them. I think they wanted me to participate in it also, but I've never did anything to people like they said they would do to the pair. I never killed anyone nor have I ever wanted too. I just wanted to earn some reward to survive on and have something to do with my time that wouldn't be harmful to others."

"Why then did you fight for them last night?"

"I didn't know who you were. You two scared the hell out of us coming out of the dark screaming and waving those knives and I didn't want to die. I want to live a peaceful and meaningful life. I'm sorry the elder got hurt bad. He's one great fighter and I'm glad I didn't have to fight him when he was younger. If the other guy hadn't been fighting with me too, I'd be dead. I knew I had to give up when the woman took down the other guy."

"His name is Troung Van Ba and he is a great warrior for the No Name. He has been most successful in all the many missions he's ever taken on, never failing. Did you hear them say anything at all about any other groups that might be waiting to ambush us in case the Mandarin failed in his task?"

"All I heard was this was their last chance to get the package and if we failed it could mean all of our deaths. I remember that a couple of times a runner came to Xinhua and passed on information about the two defeating another group north of us and also not taking the right trails, or something similar."

"You were never in contact with any other group, is that correct?"

"Yes! If they were in contact with us, I didn't know about it."

"I want you to think for a moment. Is there anything else you can tell us about the Mandarin or his gang that could help us?"

"Except that he seems to be a self-centered ass, stuck up, and sometimes acts, not only a little feminine, but like the rest of us were lowly and unworthy peasants for him to do whatever he wished to. I saw him run like the coward he is last night. I was surprised to see him tied to a tree too. I don't know anything about where he came from or who he takes his orders from. I think that he is a weakling and maybe he likes men and little boys. He refused to carry any of the gear which put more of a burden on us."

"Oh Mot, my dear lady of the knife, please come over here, would you please. I want you to tell this man what your husband has said about fighting this young one here and the other guy."

"He said the other guy was a young and a good fighter, but that you were strong and determined and he was really dumb to take on the two of you as your youth and fighting skills were very good. He thought he would collapse and leave this world at the end of your' knife. Although you're not a real bad dude, he thinks you should still fight for your pride and honor. He was surprised that you were in the Mandarin's group. You're young, strong and smart and in better shape than him and he thought it would be hard to find someone any more as talented as you in a fight."

"I'm very sorry he's hurt. I was really scared out of my wits by you people and I was only protecting myself."

Mot told him, "When he wakes, he'll be glad to see you. And I bet you'll talk about fighting moves. Let me change the subject. Let us get some rice wine and celebrate good times with him. We found some in Nguyen Phat's bag.

"What about me," Bui Tinh said" I'm hungry and thirsty and the sun beating down through the opening in the trees is not helping me."

"Da cut his arms and legs free, tie his knees together and let him sit up." He did so and the man was ecstatic and rubbing his sore wrists and ankles from the bindings. "Mot and Da bring him lots of food, tea and bread. I want the Mandarin to watch him eat and salivate. With no food and water for him he's really taking a beating from the sun. We'll let him ripen some more. Let's check on Van Ba." When the three got to him he was just waking up again. Still a little groggy from sleep, he looked at his friends and in an almost demanding tone he said, "How soon will we be getting out of here? I think I can walk ok now."

"Van Ba," the invisible One said, "this will disappoint you, but we're spending two nights here. Maybe you can walk some but those cuts will take you down. Any strain on them could start them bleeding again. I think you're more fatigued than you realize also. The day after tomorrow we will leave and your wounds will survive the travel better. We will go to Da's hamlet first to see the Bac Si (doctor) and get ointment for your wounds after they are checked. We will bathe, get new clothes, shoes, and get fresh foods and bread. We'll spend the night and start out the next morning."

Da's coming with us. Some day we may need a younger Invisible One. I think he will fit the bill after I've trained him. He's smarter and tougher than we initially thought. Tomorrow Mot will start giving him some fighting lessons. It may be fun for you to watch. The guy who surrendered to you has high praise for your skills and feels you are a great fighter and he feels very sorry for your wounds. He said he would be dead if the other guy hadn't been there to help keep you at bay."

While the two were talking Mot fixed a cup of tea and brought it and some bread to Van Ba. Then she sat beside him, put her arm around his good shoulder, and laid her head on it too. He winced a little, but he liked her being there. She had him look over at the prisoner and explained why he was sitting up with his knees tied together and added, "Our great friend here got some good information from the guy. Some of it is good news for us. The Invisible One thinks we should take him to Nguyen Hai Too. He is smart and has good skills. He feels the guy could be a big help to Nguyen Hai.

"Now then my big guy I want you to listen to me very carefully. When you have finished with your tea and bread you will lie back down and rest some more. You're going to rest, you're going to heal, and you're going to get better or else I'm going to clobber you over the head with my cooking pot. I hope you understand because I have spoken!"

Van Ba turned his head towards the Invisible on and complained, "See what I'm going to have to put up with the rest of life? I can't believe this shit. Some days it just doesn't pay to get sliced and diced up and get sympathy too."

Mot gave him little swat on the back of the head then nibbled on his ear a little.

CHAPTER 11

THE NEXT DAY THE group rested, talked and ate their fill. The rest was precious to the bodies of Van Ba, Mot, and the Invisible One too. They had pushed themselves to a nearly exhausted state since Tra Ke#4. Van Ba benefited from the rest the most due to his wounds. By the end of the day he felt much better and his wounds seemed to hurt less and so far, no signs of infection. Da left early in the morning, before sun up, for his-sub hamlet to retrieve his bullock. The plan was for Van Ba to ride it as the group made its way to Da's sub-hamlet the next day. The trio felt it would be nice to have the energy of Da's youth. The prisoners were fed and watched while they relaxed as well.

Early evening Da returned with the bullock, and with fresh bread and some vegetables. He had run all the way to the sub-hamlet and rode his animal back. He informed the Invisible One that he has arranged for hovels, a big one for Van Ba and Mot, one small one for the Invisible One and one for the prisoners along with guards. He arranged for the Hamlet Doctor to check and treat Van Ba's wounds. While they are at his sub hamlet some of the women would make new clothes for them. The women will also make sure they are well fed. There will be someone to help keep an eye on the prisoners, especially while he and the Invisible one slept. They would stay at least two days depending on the healing progress of Van Ba's wounds, but they would be welcome to stay as long as they wished.

"You are quite a worthy young man," the Invisible One told Da. "You are always full of good surprises to us. When we found you we never expected you to be such an asset to us. So, you must know by now that you are coming with us when we leave your sub-hamlet. I think that once I teach you about life and train your fighting spirit and get you some experience, you'll eventually be the next Invisible One for Nguyen Hai and the No Name."

"Do you really mean this?" Bowing and placing his hands together in front of his face he expounded, "I am so humbled by your expectations. But, how could I ever replace you? I'm just a lowly farm boy that knows only riding his buffalo, farming and nothing of the real world."

"It is as I said. I will make the change in you unless you're weak, you're cowardly, you have no will to work hard and have no desire to learn. However, if you are a strong, fearless, and a hard worker and willing to learn and to devote yourself to Nguyen Hai and the No Name, you will do well."

"Master, I am your humble servant. I pledge to you I will not be a disappointment to you. I'll work for you like no other could ever do. Your guidance will be my duty until my death."

"Don't let this go to your head. I'm not your master yet. Conical hats do not fit large melons on top of necks. Now go get yourself some much needed food and rest. We have a hard trip to make tomorrow with a wounded man and prisoners, and it will be much slower than your trip today."

Mot was getting ready to clean up the pots, the food and bowels when she saw Da coming towards her. She waved him over and placed the food back on the fire. While the food was warming, he told her of the arrangements he made and she gave him a big hug. "You would make any mother proud to have you as a son. I hope my first child is a son and that he is a copy of you. When the men first brought you into our camp, I thought you were a weak weed that would easily bend in the wind or be easily pulled from the earth by the wind, but you turned out to be a tall strong reed defying the wind and the pull on your' stalk. You have a great future ahead of you if the Invisible One has anything to do with it."

"That's okay. The important thing is that I'm very happy that you approve of me, Mot. It really means a lot to me. I've never met anyone like you before. You know, I was really worried about my future because of the Mandarin. If the truth be known I pretended to be a little weaker than I am when they caught me, but I was scared to death being taken in that manner in the middle of the night by a couple of strangers. Please don't tell the guys."

"Your secret will always safe with me. I think you and I have a special bond between us and a mutual respect that will be everlasting," she responded while dishing up some food for Da. "Eat your fill my friend. There's still plenty left and you need to keep up your strength every bit as the rest of us do. I'm sorry I didn't get a chance to teach you some fighting moves today, however, I feel the Invisible One will make up for it big time. I foresee many sore and aching muscles for you in the future."

"Oh! I'm sure he will see to it. He informed me he has plans to do just that. I feel a rough time coming up training and learning with him but I'm really looking forward to it."

"I'm so happy for you. For one such as he is to take you under his wing is a great compliment and honor to you. Mark my words Da. You do your best at it or I'll kick your butt myself, all the way to the moon and back, twice!"

"Yes, mother dear!" His grin was as bright as the new moon when he answered. Mot's Grin was even bigger. She knew she would soon have to become used to being called Mother, by several she hoped.

All was quiet throughout the camp site, and within an hour everyone was asleep except Van Ba. He rolled quietly away from Mot and stood up. He stretched and bent his body every way he could to see where he hurt the most. He was satisfied that he didn't feel very restricted in his movements even though his muscles were sore and he still had some pain in his back; his wounds did not bleed or didn't hurt as much. The last couple of days of rest had really helped him recover some. He lay back down and curled up to Mot secure in the knowledge that the trip on the marrow wouldn't be as bad as he had feared it would be. Before he drifted back to sleep, he made up his mind he wouldn't let anyone know how good he really felt, just in case something might happen along on the road. He hoped he could fake it pretty good. Mot and the guys were very perceptive.

As the sun was bringing the first glimpse of day Mot was up, had the fire going and was preparing the food as usual. After everyone was up and around, and fed, the group packed their gear and then cleaned up the area around them as much as possible. The two prisoners had their hands tied in front of their bodies, a length of rope tied to each man's thighs just above his knees. This allowed him to walk, but the rope was tied short enough above the knees that they couldn't run. Then another length of rope was made into a noose and the noose placed loosely around the necks. Van Ba who would be riding the bullock would hold the Mandarin's line and Da would hold the other prisoner's rope. The Invisible One would take the lead and Mot would walk beside Van Ba and the animal. Da and the other prisoner would bring up the rear. When they were ready Van Ba's two male friends helped him on to the animal not realizing he was faking being weaker than he was. Some of their gear was also strapped on to the animal in front of its rider too. Then the odd-looking group began their slow hike.

The sun looked to be coming out bright and warmer than it had been. That was good news for the group. It made walking a little more comfortable. The Invisible One set a slow pace that the animal could easily keep up with. The animal could go a little faster, but would tire sooner due to its heavy load. After a bit they came to the trail to Da's sub-hamlet. Mot and Van Ba talked about the beautiful sky and the surrounding country side. Van Ba remarked to his lover that on such a beautiful day they should be making beautiful love in their own home. Mot heartily agreed. Looking up at her man she felt a little horny.

After another fifteen minutes the Invisible One halted the group so they could rest a little and drink plenty of water. He didn't want anyone in the group to dehydrate. Mot held the two ropes attached to the prisoners while the two guys helped Van Ba down from his mount. He was glad to get off of it because his legs were feeling a little cramped up. He informed his friends that he would walk a little when they resumed their hike. They were against it, but he was adamant about it. The Invisible One joked that the group would see that he received a nice funeral and they would light a lot of josh sticks in his honor.

When the group felt rested and their thirst quenched, they resumed their travel. The temperature was warming more than they had expected. Van Ba felt more affected by it than he wanted to be, but as stubborn as he was, he wouldn't complain. It kept getting harder to put one foot in front of the other so he casually informed the guys fibbing,

"I think I'll try riding again. My legs aren't cramping like they were." The guys helped him mount the bullock once more. The two guys knew that he wasn't being honest about the cramps and they respected his pride and smiled inwardly. Mot had been watching him closely and decided he was as dumb not only as the animal he was riding, but as the hardest rock you could find. However, he was her dummy, her rock, her man, and she loved every minute of it.

Around noon time they stopped to rest and drink water again and eat some bread and dried fish. The whole group talked about the sun and the warmer weather which was a little odd for this time of the year, and agreed it would have been nice to have some shade trees to help cool off. Da informed them that there would be some trees up ahead and they could rest again and cool down; maybe even take a nap. That sounded good to all. Having rested for nearly an hour they loaded up began their march all over again, all of them looking forward to resting under the trees.

After trekking another two hours a grove of trees was sited. It took another one-half hour to reach it. Da being familiar with this grove led them back into a large clearing. They put down their mats and got comfortable. After a few minutes Da had collected some fire wood, started a fire and Mot put on some water to boil for tea. After some tea and bread the Invisible One stood guard while everyone napped. After a while he woke Da to stand guard while he rested. Except for those two everyone slept for about two and a half hours. When everyone was awake and slaked their thirst Da informed them that they would only have less than two more hours before they reached his sub-hamlet. If the pace of the trip hadn't been slow for the animal and Van Ba, the group would be comfortable and well taken care of all ready. All were ready to get started on the trail anew. Van Ba had Da cut a switch to prod the bullock with and insisted they pick up the pace, but just a little. All agreed. They were really anxious to spend a couple of days in a hovel for a change. They were getting tired of camping out each night.

The group was hurting physically from their quickened pace. Feet, legs and backs were burning from the exertion and their loads, even Van Ba who did get off the animal a couple of more times to walk. He decided he wasn't as physically sound as he had led himself to believe. Despite their discomfort when they observed people working in the fields it brought some elation to them knowing that soon this leg of the trek was over and they could rest, recoup their strength and regroup after a few days in comfort. A little farther down the trail they could see the hovels of the sub-hamlets.

A young man riding his bullock in the field spotted them and spurred his animal into a trot to alert the sub-hamlet that the honored travelers were approaching.

Suddenly the people started to walk up the trail to greet them and the farmers were coming from the field. When the groups met the farmers took the loads from the travelers, two hamlet security men took charge of the prisoners, and the women and boys showered the group with thanks and pats on the backs, welcoming them in every way. The chatter was so loud with the people crowding around Van Ba thought he would go deaf. The crowd hustled them into the sub-hamlet and there the Sub-Hamlet Chief, the Hamlet Chief, and the Village Chief, with their aides, were smiling and patting them on the back also while greeting them as heroes as great as all of the heroes of their country.

The travelers, very embarrassed, had never been so highly praised. It was unreal. It was as though they were returning war heroes after defeating a large invading force, but they did relish the attention. When the din quieted down each of the chiefs made a little speech and pledged all the assistance with in their capacity. This meant that their aides would be the one's doing the assisting.

Before the group were shown their quarters, they were informed that the women had food ready to be cooked, would get it started and that there would be a feast a little later. A young woman was called forth to show them their lodgings. She explained to them that the prisoners would be placed in a strongly guarded hovel next to Da's and the Invisible One's hovels, then informed Van Ba and Mot that the village doctor was waiting for them in their abode. She then guided the group to three hovels in a row. The travelers could see that the prisoners were already in one across the way and was being guarded. The Invisible One and Da waved to Van Ba and Mot and stepped in to theirs. As the young woman waved the two lovers into their hovel, she indicated that she hoped they would enjoy their stay and then she was gone. The Doctor was waiting inside and to the pair he looked and sounded a little grumpy.

I'm Bac Si Bon. Please take off your cloths and let me examine your wounds." Van Ba complied with Mot's help. The Bac Si looked at Mot sourly as if to say, "Why don't you wait outside?" Mot returned the look, took the hint, and let Bac Si Bon know that she and Van Ba shared their bodies and she would stay right there. Once his clothes were off the Dr. examined the wounds closely. He could see a little redness around them, but nothing to indicate they were infected. His diagnosis was that the wounds seemed to have begun their healing process. The Dr. carefully cleansed the wounds from a bowl of warm water. He reached into his bag filled with herbs, ointments and cutting instruments. He chose a salve and applied it to the cuts and only bandaged three of them. Very sternly the Dr. looked him in the eyes and told Van Ba, "You can put your pants on now. I'm satisfied your wounds will heal properly; however as long as you stay here, I'll come in each day to clean and apply salve to them. You must be careful not to do anything that would cause them to burst open."

"Young Da informed me that due to a long energy sapping mission and a fierce fight against two opponents you are exhausted in addition to losing a lot of blood. Take advantage of your stay here, let your wounds heal and let your body regain its strength. When I leave here, I'll let the women who will make new clothes for you know you are ready to be measured. That's why you need to put your pants back on. Good day!" He was gone.

Van Ba looked at Mot with a weird look on his face and asked her, "Is he for real?" Mot laughed at him and informed him that he would follow the Bac Si's orders or else she would put a tourniquet around his neck to stop the breathing! "Yes, my dear Mother, I'll be your enslaved son and follow the Bac Si's orders." He replied to Mot. "Just you wait till it's our bed time. I'll show you who the real boss is! You'll get some of Van Ba's special medicine, a real healing tonic. It is called Bac Si Van Ba's Sweet Elixir of Life." She sure hoped she'd get Bac Si Van Ba's Sweet Elixir of Life that night.

Two older women entered the hovel and greeted the pair, thanking them for being heroes. One woman measured Mot and the other measured Van Ba. They used a series of strings and knotted them at the proper lengths. The one with Mot told her that she would receive a nice green top and black pants and the other told Van Ba he would get black pants and a white tunic. Both women declared that the two heroes would be the best-looking couple in the sub-hamlet. The women bade their leave and went to measure the Invisible One and Da. As the two women left the young woman that had guided them to this hovel stuck her head into the entrance and informed them that the feast would be ready in about an hour and she would return to guide them to it. Van Ba finished dressing and the two sat on a mat. Van Ba, exhausted from the trip, laid his head on Mot's shoulder and was in dreamland before she could say a word. She laid her head against his and in an instance, she too drifted off and slowly they both slumped back on the mat. The next thing either of them knew was the young women gently waking them to go to the sub-hamlets feast.

The two lovers and their two friends gorged themselves on rice, fish, thinly sliced meat more or less sautéd with greens, bread, tea and then too much rice wine. The locals did dances and sang songs for the travelers. When everyone, it seemed like the whole sub hamlet, was getting inebriated, the revelry and the bacchanalia slowed down and all retreated to their abodes for the night.

The young woman once again escorted the lovers to their quarters and departed. Their mat and blankets were already in place so they hurriedly shrugged off their clothes and quickly entwined themselves under the blankets. Now there was nothing to worry about except each other and their love making was unabated throughout the early hours of the night. Exhausted, they finally fell dead to the world and didn't wake until mid-morning. They didn't know that the young woman had looked in on them to be sure they were okay. They greeted the day with a passionate kiss and dressed. They were eager to find out what was in store for them this day. They hoped it would be like it was after they reached the sub-hamlet. It was humbling to be treated so wonderfully.

As they were about to exit the hovel the Bac Si came in the entrance. His first words were, "Take off the clothes so I can check the wounds. If you'd have been up at a decent time this morning, we could have had this checkup done with. I don't know about some of you guys." Van Ba obeyed without mentioning what he really wanted to tell the Dr. to do, like take a flying leap off a high cliff. Mot was sent to get some warm water to wash off the old salve and clean the wounds. When that task was done more salve was administered. After that the Bac Si bade them a good day and went on his rounds or whatever.

When the pair exited, both in their old dirty and ragged clothes, they saw that the young woman was squatting quietly on her haunches across the path from their hovel. She greeted them and informed them that she would go and bring some food and tea and that it would take her about fifteen minutes, then she was on her way. The pair just walked hand in hand a short way looking around the sub hamlet and enjoying the mid-morning sun. As they returned to the hovel the young woman was arriving with a tray of food, a younger girl behind her had a tray with hot tea and cups, and behind her was an older woman carrying the couple's new clothes. Both Van Ba and Mot were astonished. Neither one had ever had such wonderful treatment.

The young girl and the older woman left the tea and clothes, but the young woman sat in the corner and told the lovers, as they ate, why the people were so ecstatic about the heroes being there and honoring them.

"First let me say that I am honored that an unworthy one as I was chosen to serve you. We have never had any one fighting for our sub-hamlet knowingly or unknowingly before. Our men are farmers who work the fields. They are not fighters." Then she addressed Van Ba as he was the male. "Let me tell you our story."

"This is what happened in our sub hamlet a few days ago. The Mandarin and his gangsters came to our sub hamlet looking for Da early one morning. He was in the field working so the criminals tried stealing from the hovels. The people didn't have any worthwhile personal possessions to steal so they beat up some children and raped some of the women and young girls that were in their abodes. I don't think Da knew about that. What they did manage to steal was rice, bread and tea and I don't know what else. The Men in the fields didn't know what was happening or that everyone here was scared for their lives. When Da returned from the field they forced him to go with them. We thought we would never see him alive again. Some of the men wanted to follow and attack kill them and rescue Da, however the Hamlet Chief reminded the men that they had no fighting skills, they did not know which direction the gang went, and there was too much work to be done in the fields. Not only were the people in our sub-hamlet, but the people in the rest of the Hamlet's sub-hamlets were saddened by this event."

"No one thought we'd ever see Da again, especially me. Then the morning that Da returned and told of your heroics, and yours too Mot, really excited the people. It was hard to believe that a young beautiful woman such as yourself could be a great fighter too. He told me this morning of the things you did. He really looks up to you. With hearing about the capture of the Mandarin and one of his henchmen and the killing of the rest of the gang everyone here rejoiced. Many cried happy tears, many laughed, many jumped up and down. It was a great day for us. No one had ever avenged us before."

"Da told us what your group needed and of the need of a Bac Si for you. Every soul here, even the children wanted to help you for avenging the ravishing of our women and children. The Village and Hamlet leaders decided what was to be done, by whom, and instructed Da to bring all of you here as soon as you were able to travel. Da was instructed not to tell you of the incident here and that you would be told at the proper time after you were fed and rested."

"Your friend the Invisible One and Da are being cared for the same as you. I think the young woman assisting them likes the Invisible One. She blushes each time she speaks of him. The people here feel they have been smiled upon by their ancestors to have him here. His reputation is well known to all. The prisoners are being well guarded and fed. The men guarding them would like to torture and kill them, but they took an oath they would not harm them unless they tried to escape. Now, if you have any questions, I'll be glad to answer them in my humble way if I can."

Van Ba looked at Mot as though to say you begin and she did. "Could I meet with the women and young girls, maybe as a group, who were raped and offer my sympathy and encouragement to them? We did not know of the tragedy here but we are so glad our actions brought good feelings to the people. If we would have known about the situation we could have been meaner to them, like cutting their cock and balls off and sticking them in their mouth, just for the heck of it."

Blushing the young girl said, "I'd have loved to see that. To answer your question, I think I could get the women and children to gather to have a talk."

"Van Ba interrupted with, "Why not assemble the whole sub hamlet including the men. All four of us want to praise them for all of the good things being done for us. Our travel has been arduous and our bodies worn down. We really appreciate everything being done for us. If we had been here, we would have fought for you in an instance."

The young woman had an immediate solution. "I'll have one meeting with Mot, the women and the children, and then have a sub-hamlet meeting with all the people and you four. I think it will work out fine. The people do want to hear from you. They will want to know the story blow by blow and how the scum died, bravely or cowardly. It will be informative and satisfy some of the warrior dreams they have. They don't really have weapons and can't fight very well, but they can identify with your story. In their minds they are slaying the vermin too. They look to you as their Heroes and Avengers. You will always have friends here. By the way, Mot, the women and children are awed and look up to you in the same way as they do as your men. You are their heroin."

"Everyone here is amazed at you Van Ba. They cannot imagine how any warrior could survive such a battle and with such wounds as you have after having such a long and arduous journey. They wish you a speedy recovery and a speedy return to your old fighting prowess. I feel the same way as they do and I bow to you too." She stood, placed her palms together in front of her face and bowed, with her head down, from the waist to him. "The history of our sub-hamlet will always remember and celebrate you as they have all the Vietnamese Heroes and Heroines over the ages."

"You needn't bow to me girl, it humbles me too much. I only did what my duty demanded of me. I must admit that I had a duty to complete a mission to the No Name, but more than that make sure that Mot was kept safe and sound, for she may have my child someday. My only wish is that my friends and I could have been here to stop the chaos the people here had to suffer. I can feel the people's angst in my own old bones. If we had known the situation here I would have fought more fiercely along with my companions. I am humbled by the people's concern for our physical wellbeing and their generosity to us. It is as I said, it's very humbling."

To the young woman Mot stated, "That's my man. I am so lucky to have him and I hope you find a man as worthy as he is and you can share many happy events throughout your lives together." She went on to say, "We have had many adventures on our journey, but we will look back at our stay here as the high light of it. The adoration shown to us by you and the people here will always brighten our days spent in the sun. It is the most remarkable thing to ever happen to us. I hope everyone here realizes that we could not have tasted victory if not for Da's actions. We were very surprised at his performance under pressure. A cool head rests on his shoulders. He will leave here with the Invisible One when we go to train for a position with the No Name, but your people need to remember him always. Someday he'll be a great patriot for you to be proud of."

Mot noticed that when she mentioned Da's name the young woman blushed a bit and smiled a lovely smile. Being as perceptive as she was, Mot knew immediately that the young woman liked Da; a lot. In that case Da probably liked her as well. They might even be in love or just in lust. Maybe she could do something about it whichever it was. She would make it her business to bring two love birds together for a life time if she could.

CHAPTER 12

THE MEETING WITH MOT, the women and children and then the meeting with all of the inhabitants with the four went very well. The people overwhelmed the Heroes with their gratitude, praise and attention they had given them. The people there were all thankful not only for the advice given on healing their mental wounds, but some physical wounds from the attacks. The foursome then promised the people that if they were ever needed for protection or whatever, to send for them immediately and they would repay the kindness they had received, no matter what the need might be.

The next morning the Invisible One, after checking on the prisoners, sent a messenger from the sub hamlet to a place known only to him. Nguyen Hai would be there with his entourage, his security team, and waiting on, he hoped, good news of the Jade Cross and the secret document. It would take the messenger nearly two whole days to get there. On the morning of the third day he would start out with his group and meet up with Nguyen Hai at a halfway-point.

They would meet the messenger along the way back with the location. This would give Van Ba two more days to rest up. He seemed to be recovering very well from his wounds and strengthening of his worn-down body. Of course, his relationship, not only just the sex, with Mot, had certainly helped him. It gave him a reason to heal quickly, to love, and not feel sorry for his self over his wounds. Sometimes recovering from wounds could be very depressing and was not good for an individual. Van Ba seemed above allowing a depression to befall him.

The Invisible One's message noted that the Jade Cross and the document were safe with Van Ba and Mot. It briefly noted the two fights, the prisoners and the injuries to Van Ba and that he was recovering very well. He knew that Nguyen Hai would be delighted to know how the team had protected the Jade Cross, the secret document, and had the Mandarin in custody, but he kept that information about the Mandarin being one of the prisoners to his self so that he could surprise Nguyen Hai. He did note that he may have found his eventual future replacement in the young Da. Until he retired, two Invisible Ones could do twice the job in half the time. Thinking of that made him feel good. There was a lot of training ahead for the young one. Da would feel aches and pains that Da didn't even know was possible but it would be well worth it for him. Da would build an inner toughness as well as a strong body and fighting skills, as well as the mental endurance and quick thinking at performing tough but needed acts for the No Name for years.

Da felt a little down so he went to Van Ba and Mot that morning and spoke to them of his major dilemma. The young woman that was the host to Van Ba and Mot he liked very much. They had grown up together and in fact he believed he was very much in love with her, and she with him. He wanted to bring her along with them on the trip to meet Nguyen Hai and marry her someday. His problem was that he was afraid to ask the Invisible One for permission to bring her along. He still felt a little intimidated by his new mentor and asked them to intercede on his behalf with the Invisible One. Mot asked him why it was important for him to bring her along when she could wait for him at the sub hamlet and keep the home fires burning while he was away.

He answered her truthfully and firmly, "I think I would kill myself if I had to leave this sub hamlet alone. I just don't want to live without her. I've never felt this way about any woman before. I know that she feels the same as I do. We've never made love or anything else yet, but we are both ready to make a life together and raise a big family."

"Van Ba started to say something, but Mot hushed him. "Da, this old decrepit man and I both understand your feelings, don't we old and decrepit man?" She stared at her man and he wisely crossed his arms and nodded a yes. "When he and I first met we didn't like each other much. I thought he was a dumb stupid ass and he thought he had no need for me. Sharing hardships together did change how we felt about each other and it enriched our lives so very much. We can never part from each other now. Marriage is one of the priorities for us too. We will talk to the Invisible One for you and her and give you a good recommendation to him; wont we dearest one?" She crossed her arms across her breasts, tapped her right foot, and looked sharply at Van Ba.

"Yes, my Empress. Your very wish is my command." He bowed to her with his hands together in front of his face. "I pledge an oath to you the same as if you were one of the Honorable Trung Sisters, Trung Trac and Trung Nhi."

She smiled and giggled at him. "You're funny old man." Then she turned to Da and promised him, "I will drag this un-honorable and worthless vagabond peasant of mine with me to the Invisible One and we will present your cause of love to him. I'm sure he will want to keep you happy."

"I spoke to your young woman earlier about marriage and told her I hoped she found a good man like mine to marry. I didn't know it would be you. You're a good choice for her. I know she will be treated the way a woman should be treated, by you, or I'll kick your butt from here to the moon and back!"

She put her arm around Van Ba's waist, laid her head on his chest and continued, "I'm a very lucky woman to have such a great man. I'm very proud of him and for myself to be so lucky. I believe you and her will both be very lucky to have one another in wedded bliss. I wish many wonderful children and many grandchildren for you two also. I know they will be raised to be honorable and responsible individuals like you and her."

Van Ba only smiled at her praise of him. He was learning to keep quiet as a woman's man must always do at certain times to protect his shins from what he laughing called, a Mot kick. Da thanked them very much and left, then the lovers went to find the Invisible One and make their plea for him.

They found the Invisible Man squatting behind the hovel he was staying in, whittling a new walking/fighting staff from a sapling that one of the young boys had gotten for him. As they approached him Mot made it clear to Van Ba that she would do the talking. He was thinking, and not aloud, "Isn't that what she's been doing since I met her. She's been talking all the time!" He laughed to himself at the thought of her talking. He had quite a woman on his hands. When they were next to him Mot cleared her throat and greeted him, "Good morning my dear and cherished friend. How are you today?"

"Good morning to you both, my friends. How are you healing Van Ba? I hope it's in the best way and you'll be ready to travel in two days. I have sent word out to Nguyen Hai by messenger and we'll leave in three days to meet with him."

"Mot, you're looking very lovely as usual. I know you well enough right now that I'll bet that you're giving such a greeting to me and Van Ba being so quiet means you want something from me, am I right? You do look guilty, he responded with a big smile."

A little red faced, a blushing Mot agreed that, "I guess you do know me very well. I wear my heart on my sleeve sometimes. I guess it's the female in me. My worthless companion and I have come to speak to you as a favor for Da. It's something that he feels very important to him and his future life by going or not going with you when we leave here."

"I'm a little ahead of you there. I've watched Da and I believe he's head over heels in love with a certain young woman here, and as a matter of fact, the one who has been attending to your' needs. Now my only question is, what exactly does he need me to do for him that he can't do for himself?"

Van Ba giggled at Mot and received a kick in the left shin for his panning her as she was at a loss for words and that the Invisible One was one step ahead of her. She wondered how he managed to do it, but she continued as though he had said nothing.

"Da and a young woman, the one you mentioned, are in love. They have been for some time now. Neither one desires a long-distance relationship. Da would like to bring her along and marry her. I think it's not only his love, but a certain part of the brain in his pants that needs to do this also. He swears that it will motivate his worthless soul to work even harder for you. So, I implore you to consider his plea this day."

The Invisible One couldn't help but to laugh long and hard. "Mot, you are a real jewel amongst the gems. I've anticipated this and already have an answer. I think it's a good idea and I have no problem with it. I don't want you to tell him he has my permission to bring her. When you see him again, tell him he must come to me and ask this favor for himself. I will keep him in suspense a bit. It will be the first lesson I will give him as my trainee. A person must always speak up for his self, and, no disrespect to you, Mot, and not ask a woman to do it for you. I am glad though that he trusts you to speak for him. He shows good sense in the giving of his trust to you and your' husband to be. Van Ba, you're very quiet and looking a little sheepish this morning. Has a tiger got your tongue?"

"Oh my, yes. This ferocious female tiger beside me has got my tongue!" His left shin received another swift kick, this one had him hopping on his right leg, holding his left shin and groaning."

"Serves you right," she retorted. "This ferocious crouching tiger is going to eat you alive, lover boy." Then she growled at him and giggled, Van Ba blushed.

Van Ba then asked the Invisible One, "Do you have a long, sharp knife?" This time he was able to dodge the kick in the same shin and he laughed then grabbed Mot giving her a big hug and a quick kiss. This action calmed the ferocious crouching tiger in her to a meow.

"You're acting like a couple of rabbits. I think you two need to get back to your hovel and make up for lost time there. There are times that love cannot be delayed, nor hurried even for Da and his woman. Thanks for coming my friends."

The lovers bid him a good day and left, meandering along with their arms around the others waist. Van Ba whispered in her ear, "Now instead of being a ferocious tiger you're going to be miss tame rabbit. Did you know that the man rabbit always jumps on the back of the woman rabbit?" Mot smiled at him and nodded her head in agreement. He thought of Wham Bam Thank You Maam.

After they went a few more steps Mot whispered to him, "You know this could take you from being number ten thousand to number one if you play your cards right. Oh, I forgot that we don't have any cards, but I guess you can deal me in any way. Maybe even deal me face down like a hole card."

"I'm not going to be dealing or playing any cards. I'm going to deal and play you and your body like a fine musical instrument and you'll soon be cooing like a dove."

"She answered him with Coo! Coo!"

"Damn, let's hurry up. I want you so very bad."

Along the path they saw Da and stopped. Van Ba, with a brain storm, called him over to them and in a stern voice informed Da that, "The Invisible One wants to see you right now, on the double. He's as ticked off as can be. You must be prepared to explain why you want to take the woman with you and marry her! Go on and hurry off to see him now." Mot said not a word, but was smiling inside.

Da answered with a, "Yes sir," turned and hastily strode quickly towards his new master's hovel.

When Da was far enough away not to hear her, Mot kicked Van Ba playfully in the shin again, and quipped, "You are one mean old ogre!" Then, they both laughed and hurried to their love nest.

They had just gotten their clothes back on when the young woman brought them lunch. Mot related to her about how the Invisible One approved of her going with Da, and how her worthless tag-a-long had tricked Da into thinking the Invisible one was angry with him and he scurried off thinking he had displeased his new Master. The young woman giggled with a big smile, and thanked them from the bottom of her heart and left them to their meal.

Awhile after eating lunch the pair went for another walk around the sub-hamlet. They came across their two friends and Da said to Van Ba, "I should cut you down here and now with my long knife, but then this wonderful woman would cut off a certain part of my body I'm sure she craves to do and that wouldn't do for you, would it. You had me scared out of my wits Van Ba. It is funny though."

"I couldn't resist it. Being fooled is sometimes a good thing when you're young. It adds to your learning of the games that people play. It helps to carve and sharpen your perspective on life and make you more vigilant to your evaluation of people and things they say and do, with you and for you. Besides, wait till you have many children. There will be times you must fool them so they can learn and have great fun with them while doing it doing it. I can remember my foster dad fooling me many times and I learned a lot from it."

"Well now! I'll tell you what, you old goat, I will let you off the hook this time. I did learn a lesson from it. I have to speak up for myself and not burden my friends over my personal duty. I need to thank you for speaking to my master about the young woman. I'm forever in your debt. Thank you, Mot!"

"The thank you does belong to Mot. She alone, as I was not allowed to speak, was the one who spoke to your new master in favor of your pending marriage, and she hasn't stopped talking yet." He just managed to avoid a good kick in the other shin.

"Oh, you're despicable, you old demon. Da, I did speak to him for you, however he was ahead of me and was already in favor of you and your young woman. You should thank your new master if you haven't already, and have your sweetheart do likewise. Remember that if you ever do need our help for anything, please do ask us for it. We are your friends, forever and ever and don't you forget it."

"I did thank him. I will seek your council when and if I really need it. I must to learn to cope with things on my own if I am to become a future Invisible One. Now I must go and speak to her so she can prepare for the journey."

Van Ba said before Da could leave, "I started this journey by myself. Then there were two of us, then three, then four, and now there is five. This mission gets better all the time."

Mot, with a cherubic smile replied to this that, "Maybe there are six of us." The others looked at her with the weirdest look on their face. "I hope this is so." Van Ba's face lit up and thought aloud, "Maybe, I'm going to be a father?'"

Knowing what must be going through her lover's mind, blushing, she added, "I'm not real sure yet, but I think so daddy."

All three men hugged her and offered their hope for a sixth member of the crew. Van Ba couldn't resist rubbing her stomach with a big assed grin. "I think it feels like a boy. I feel something sticking up." They all had a good laugh and went their own ways, the lovers walking hip to hip each with an arm around the other and thankful for their new-found lives and future happiness and a family blessed by Buda.

The next day the Invisible One gathered the group together, now including the young woman, and explained to them the message to Nguyen Hai and that they would eat an early morning breakfast the next day then leave for the rendezvous. He instructed them to gather food and water and whatever else that was needed and have it ready when they turned in for the night as it would save time in the morning. They would have to carry their own gear because

Da had given his water buffalo to the young woman's father for her hand. He also noted that the people would be assembled because they wanted to bid them goodbye. He also informed Van Ba that, "The Sub-Hamlet chief said that the people were happy that he was able to recover from his wounds so quickly and that he would always be in their hearts for his bravery."

For most of the day after getting their gear together the group relaxed and took things easy. Of course, the lovers took advantage of part of the day and nearly wore themselves out. Later, in the afternoon the little market place was visited by the lovers and their normal fare for the trip was purchased. One of the old women who sold bread was almost out and it was a couple of days old and was starting to harden somewhat. She accepted their Dong and promised to have fresh bread for them in time for them to start their trip in the morning. She even said she would give them some extra bread for their heroism, and maybe something sweet to eat with their tea.

Their gear was all packed up except for their mats and blankets to sleep on that night, and they turned in early after meeting with the rest to make sure the plans hadn't changed. The next day would be long and somewhat tiring once more, but it would be well worth it because it was the start of the end of their mission.

When the lovers awoke the young woman was there with hot tea, bread and rice. Before they were done with the meal the old woman brought them the promised fresh, and hot, bread and some sweets. After they finished eating, they went outside with their gear and met up with the rest of the travelers. The prisoners were already to go too. They had a noose around their necks, hands tied behind them and a short rope just above the knees that would keep them from running. The people were already assembled, thanking them and fondly bidding them a safe journey. When they finally got on their way the Invisible One and Da held the prisoner's nooses. There was only a slight hint of the coming day break in the eastern sky. The five were in a good mood, the two prisoners weren't happy at all, and felt that their bodies had conquered their exhaustion and they set a good pace that would not be too tiresome.

Van Ba felt better than he had at the beginning of his mission. The few days of rest he had rejuvenated him as well as Bac Si Mot's prescribed treatment. He was well rested and his wounds were infection free and healing even faster than he had hoped they would. He was also elated at the thought of becoming a father to Mot's child. He knew how lucky he was to have such a marvelous woman for his child's mother and his future bride. His ancestors were really smiling down on him. When he thought of losing his wife and the life he led afterward and before meeting Mot, he knew it was so drab and lonely. He never wanted to go back to that kind of existence ever again. The part that surprised him the most was that he never realized that was how he had lived his worthless life.

Mot's feelings paralleled Van Ba's. Her life had also been pretty lonely and drab, with no real hope for the future. She just existed from guiding job to job. Now she has found the perfect man for her husband to be and the father to her children that she planned to have. She didn't really like him at first, but suddenly she got this feeling that he was all she wanted and needed. The more they traveled together the more wonderful traits and qualities she found in him. He was tough, rugged, smart, kind and gentle. Happiness and a wonderful life, she believed, and was her future with him. She also liked that he knew who his boss is.

Midmorning found them taking a short breather along the trail without the need to hide and drinking some water to stay hydrated. Even though their gear seemed a little heavier their bodies were not feeling achy from the burden due to the restful stay at Da's sub-hamlet. There were no signs of aching backs and tiring leg muscles or sore feet. They talked about their time resting at Da's sub hamlet and praised the people there for their generosity and reaching out to them. The heartfelt thanks by the people there had humbled them to no end. It also gave them a sense of self-esteem that had not been part of their character before. They even felt a little heroic.

Van Ba and Mot kind of embarrassed the young woman by heaping praise on her for all she did for them. Da gave her a big hug. "That's my woman!" Da whispered into her ear. Then they were off once more, continuing their hike, laughing, joking, capering and enjoying the scenery and guiding their prisoners who still were not very happy with the group.

Occasionally they would see peasants working in the fields when passing inhabited areas and once in a while a lonely traveler. Two times they shared some food with one as the men had no money or food and seemed to be malnourished. They left them feeling that there were some nice people in this world. The group felt good that they were able to share with the needy.

After the long day's trek, the group was beginning to feel some tiredness and some aches as it was getting close to sunset when they settled in for the night. They had come across a nice treed area and moved far enough into it that a fire in a small clearing would not be noticed from the road in case there were wondering bandits in the area. Mot and the young woman prepared the evening meal and after eating their fill they all turned in for the night, although the three men would each take a turn standing guard on the prisoners, so they would be able to get an early start in the morning. Van Ba volunteered to take the first watch so he and Mot could talk before she slept.

They finally believed that the end of the mission was near and they could seriously talk about Mot's pregnancy and begin to make marriage plans. They decided that after passing on the Jade Cross and the secret document their first goal was finding a place to live and then checking on a Bac Si or a midwife, to give Mot advice on her condition and aid Mot in child birth. Their number two goal would be to find a source of income. He could grow rice or be a vegetable grower or whatever. Number three would be getting married. They also realized that things may not come in the order they would like, but they would be happy however it turned out. Being together was the most important thing in their lives. Before long Mot, feeling a little groggy went to sleep and soon Da relieved Van Ba and he crawled in next to Mot, pulled her close with his arm around her and slept like a baby that might be coming several months later. He dreamed of holding an infant son close to his chest.

It was nearly dawn and the Invisible One, who had the third watch, rekindled the fire and woke the two women so they could prepare a meal. He then closed his eyes and slept till the food was ready. When the food and tea was prepared, the men were awakened and they ate their fill of it, then fed and watered the prisoners. This time the prisoner's hands were untied and they were able to feed themselves instead of having to be fed by the others as they were the night before, then the hands were retied. Then the group packed up the gear and hit the trail anew. Van Ba and Mot were really happy because this would be the day they had longed for and by day's end they would only have to worry about each other and maybe, a baby, not a Jade Cross or document.

The countryside began to take on a different persona. There were more small populated areas, more fields being farmed, more water buffalos, and they could see more rice paddies in the distance. The weather was slightly warmer and they could see signs of recent rains. Men pulling baskets through a pond or stream to catch fish fascinated Mot. She had never paid attention to men fishing before. She and the young woman talked about how nice it must be to live in places like this. They both imagined that the hamlets must have big markets and how wonderful it would be to shop them. They plotted to tell the men later about what kind of area they would like to live in. The men however interrupted their dreams and informed them it was time for a break. The sun was high in the sky when the group stopped alongside the trail and once again the women prepared the meal. The men filled the water bladders from a nearby stream. While they were eating a man was coming up the trail from the direction they were heading. As he neared the Invisible One recognized him as the messenger he had sent to Nguyen Hai. He hailed the man and they greeted each other.

The messenger informed the group that Nguyen Hai would meet them the next morning instead of that day as he had to finish a bit of business before he started out. He explained to them that about an hour before sundown they would reach a hamlet called Bin Son and that he was to guide them to it. The Hamlet Chief would meet them and give them quarters for the night and provide food and pass on any messages he might receive from Nguyen Hai. Nguyen Hai and his group should arrive about midmorning the next day. He also informed them that Nguyen Hai wished to convey his thanks on successfully completing their mission. They thanked the messenger for his service. Always knowing what to do, Mot invited the Invisible

One's messenger to sit down, rest, and share their food and he was happy to oblige her.

Van Ba wondered to his self that now there were six of them, maybe seven with a baby, about how sometimes life changed for the better. He would never have thought starting out by himself, as one, that there would even be two, let alone this many. The more the merrier he thought to himself. This is really great. He quipped to the group, "Hey everybody. Do you all think we that we might even grow to be seven or even eight vagabonds?" The rest of them just looked at him and laughed.

A lot of the people they passed looked at them suspiciously. Very seldom did the people see a large group moving up the trail that was not up to no good, especially a group leading prisoners on a noose. A wave of the hand would be given by the group to people who were working close to the trail. Sometimes it would be returned, and sometimes not. Once, two men coming up the trail towards them moved way off the trail and watched the group closely as they passed by. It was not unusual for a gang of thieves to be prowling the area. The group thought that maybe the men were bad men and wanted nothing to do with a group that outnumbered them, six to two.

In the mid-afternoon they took their final break of the day. They snacked on bread and water and a quarter of an hour later were on their way again. They finally reached Bin Son Hamlet and true to the messenger's words were met by the Hamlet Chief, Dinh Nghia. He greeted them warmly and put himself at their disposal. He informed them that there were no new messages from Nguyen Hai. He gave separate thatched hovels, one to Van Ba and Mot, and one to Da and his woman. The other three he lodged together in the same large one. He informed them that there would be someone to attend them during their stay. He provided security and a hovel for the prisoners even though he didn't know about them until the group's arrival. They were informed that in a short while an evening meal would be brought to them and of course if anything else was needed they should seek him out personally. He explained to them where he lived and how it was his humble duty to serve them by any means at his disposal.

Van Ba and Mot were standing outside their assigned hovel, the sun was just dropping below the horizon and Mot pointed out to her lover how beautiful the sun set was this night. It was the best one she'd seen recently. She assured him it meant that good things were to come to them from it. While they were enjoying it a couple of older women brought their meal and they went inside to feast. After the dishes were collected, they laid out their sleeping mats and blankets and for a long while just did what lovers do. Eventually they fell into an exhausted, but happy sleep in each other's arms. The next day would be the start of their new lives.

The sun was already rising when they were awakened by a different and older woman bringing them rice, bread and tea. Mot, still naked held a blanket in front of her and directed the woman where to set the food. As the woman left, she woke her mate and they sampled what was so wonderful the night before, then dressed and ate. Mot felt a little queasy after eating, but she didn't really get sick. She knew it wouldn't be long before she would be getting morning sickness. She was getting anxious to give Van Ba his first child. The old woman came by to pick up the dishes and left.

The two lovers went out and walked around the area just to see what it was like. Along the path they found the Invisible one talking with the Chief and another man. When he saw Van Ba and Mot, he left the two and greeted the pair. He informed them that the guy with the Chief was a runner from Nguyen Hai. Our leader should be here just before the sun is highest in the sky. Mot jumped up and down a couple of times while clapping her hands and giving a low shout of, "Yes!" Van Ba bowed to her.

The sun was nearly at its peak when a man went to each hovel and informed the group that Nguyen Hai was almost there and to assemble by the hamlet headquarters. The prisoners were already present when they arrived. Van Ba carried the Jade Cross, wrapped in its protective cloth, and the secret document. Mot, Da and his woman were a little nervous, but were ready also. The Invisible One stood tall, no sign of nerves. Finally, Nguyen Hai and his three associates and seven guards approached them. His group stopped ten feet away and he signaled his group to stay put. He stepped to the Invisible One and they embraced and exchanged pleasantries. He then greeted Da and his woman and thanked them for their service to the cause. He turned to Mot, took her hands in his and gave her his heartfelt thanks for her participation in the success of Van Ba's mission.

"Mot, I knew you would be the right one to fire up the cantankerous old Van Ba and keep him inline and motivated. You'll always be remembered for the many hardships you have endured. Maybe someday there will be annual festivals to salute your courage and devotion to the cause."

"I accept your gratitude even though I am unworthy of your praise."

"That's nonsense my dear." He turned to Van Ba who then un-wrapped the Jade Cross and proudly held it out to Nguyen Hai. Nguyen Hai looked at it with awe, carefully inspected it, gave a sigh of relief, and motioned one of his associates to come forward and he rewrapped and handed the sacred relic to him. The man stepped back to his group with it. Then Van Ba gave him the sealed document.

Then he and Van Ba embraced and praised each other. "Van Ba, my dear friend, I knew you were the right man for the job. I cannot begin to fathom the hardships, lonely days and nights, and the obstacles that you had to overcome along with your wounds. You are the essence of a true Vietnamese warrior and patriot. You have never failed the No Name or me. We'll talk about the reward for your success during the feast tonight. You will not be disappointed in the least, my old friend."

Van Ba bowed showing due respect to Nguyen Hai and stated, "I am only the servant to my dear friend and leader. I have pledged my life to the No Name and have been proud to serve. If I may speak frankly, my mission couldn't have been a success without Mot. She was so brave and solid in her actions. I owe her not only for a successful completion of the task, but she also saved my life. The only reward that I seek is for the beautiful Mot and I to marry and be allowed to raise a family."

Nguyen Hai looked at Mot and she rubbed her stomach in a circular motion. Looking at Van Ba he happily quipped, "It looks like you've got a head start on the family, you old goat. You and Mot have all of my blessings. I was thinking of letting you retire as you are getting to be an old fart, as old as the dried-up earth our fore bearers trod, but loyal and faithful. The reward I have in mind will include your future wife. I'm looking forward to the dumb founded look on your face when I reveal it to you. We'll talk later. Right now, my group and I need to eat and rest."

They nodded assent and at that time the Invisible One motioned for the prisoners to be brought forward. "I have a present for you my master."

"What is this?" Nguyen Hai looked at each one quizzically.

The Invisible one started with the gang member. "This guy was forced to go along with our enemies and he's the only one, of a few left alive, and not of his own choosing. He may be a viable convert to your endeavors and maybe very helpful to you in the long run. He's also a decent fighter. This unworthy and scrupulous one who stinks of bowel movement, is my present to you. He's a Chinese Mandarin who had foolishly planned to ambush us along the trail and steal the Jade Cross."

"We beat them to the punch where they had settled in for the night. These two are the remains of the ambush party. Nguyen Phat and Trich Tuy are no longer a concern to us. They've been greeted by their ancestors, if their ancestors would have them, and Phat becoming one with the grass. It was during that same fight in which Van Ba was severely wounded and became exhausted that Mot and Da captured the Chinese Mandarin."

Nguyen Hai gave a big smile. "This is truly a great day for me and the No Name. You are, without a doubt, the greatest warriors this country could ever ask for. Without true warriors like you, and the others, we could never have a chance to reunite our people. We'll talk a little more later on." With that he turned to the Hamlet Chief, greeted him anew and asked to be shown his and his entourage lodging and receive a small meal. Van Ba's group retired to their hovels and Nguyen Hai's security took control of the prisoners.

At the feast that night, true as he had promised, Nguyen Hai related what the reward was to Van Ba, and indeed it did entail his future life with Mot. It entailed some riches, some land, some type of status, and could not but, include a marriage ceremony as well as his and Mot's retirement. There may even be a surprise or two to boot.

Van Ba, his mouth wide open, was astounded at hearing the details of his reward, could not believe his ears, and so was Mot who was listening to, but did not hear parts of the conversation. She wanted to leap at Nguyen Hai and hug him tight. However, she knew she had to stay in her place as Vietnamese women weren't allowed to show emotions around men in situations such as this. Like little children they should be seen and not heard. So, she decided she would jump Van Ba's bones later that night, coercing him to tell her what Nguyen Hai had said.

After the feast was over Nguyen Hai told Van Ba to go on to his quarters, as he needed to speak to Mot alone for a few minutes. Van Ba bowed, bid his leave, and did as he was instructed. Nguyen Hai motioned to her and took Mot's arm and walked slowly with her towards her hovel, speaking to her all the way.

"Mot, my dearest one! There is something I must inform you about. I need you to understand about Vietnamese men of status, position, and prestige. Even though they are married they may have a concubine or two and the woman or women have to be acceptable to the Nobles wife. There are times during the wife's time of the month and or child birth or sickness when he needs to be satisfied by a woman. I know Van Ba loves you and wants to be with only you, but if he were to become a man of stature, a noble one, I must ask, would you be comfortable if he had just one concubine that would pose no threat to your marriage and could be of great service to you and to your family over the years to come?"

Mot didn't hesitate in her answer. "I know of the Vietnamese custom. I may not agree with it, but I accept it for what it is. I have anticipated that that would be a part of our life together from time to time. I want him to be sexually satisfied when he needs to be and if I can't do it myself, I would want it to be with someone who can be trusted and is not as dependent on sex as I am now. He has taught me many ways to satisfy him with different parts of my body, but I know there will be times he needs the center of the universe and that I cannot provide it. I know he will need the release of stress when I cannot provide it."

"You are wise beyond your years Mot. Trust me in that I would not put a young nymph in his path. I have a plan I will reveal to you and him later. I believe the three of us will be satisfied with it. He may not want to hear of the arrangement at this time because of his feelings for you, but I will explain it to him that it will be expected of him. Here is your place. Go to your man, I'm sure he's getting horny and I bet you are too." She entered and he was horny. She was too.

EPILOG OF VAN BA AND MOT

MOT, WHO WAS A very good-looking young woman to begin with, looked absolutely stunning, radiant and ravishing wearing the finest Ao Dai[4] she had ever seen. It was of a shimmering blue silk with a green dragon print breathing a red and yellow flame, running, in the front, from the neck to the bottom of the dress and had lotus blossoms, the traditional flower of Vietnam, printed around the dragon. Her long black hair, flowing beneath her pink khan dong[5] was nearly to her hips and was clean and shiny. The hip length slits on each side of the dress exposed her long white pants. Her pregnancy was now beginning to show somewhat and her beautiful eyes betrayed her happiness.

Van Ba could not believe his eyes. Mat Trang[6], could never out shine or be more beautiful than Mot when it was at its fullest. Was this really the rag tag women he wanted nothing to do with when first he met her? The fact that he was the luckiest guy in the world was not to be questioned by anyone or they would answer to him.

---

4   Traditional Long Dress.
5   Head dress.
6   The moon.

Van Ba wore the traditional men's Ao Dai. His was aqua colored with small green dragon patterns, and gold braid around the high collar, the cuffs of the sleeves, and around the bottom hem. The braid consisted of straight lines and small loops making him appear to be royalty. He had never worn a man's Ao Dai in his life and now dressed in this one he felt like royalty. Mot was looking at him as starry eyed as he was at her. In just a few minutes their wedding ceremony and feast would begin and they would be together as a family.

Nguyen Hai was as good as his word. When he had told Van Ba what his reward was Van Ba couldn't believe his ears. His first comment to Nguyen Hai was that, "I'm only a humble servant to the No Name's cause of reuniting the Vietnamese people and keeping the Chinese out. I've only done my duty and I am not worthy of your praise or this wonderful reward you're offering to me and Mot. We are not deserving of it."

Nguyen Hai's response was made with a smile. "Be still now or I will think you are a crazy man. You two have suffered mentally and physically, especially you, in completing your assignment. The Jade Cross will be the greatest of rallying icons, but the confidential letter on Chinese intentions is the most valuable. Had our enemy been able to retrieve the letter from you it could have been disastrous to our Cause, and caused trouble with the Chinese. I've already sent it by messenger to the Emperor. You two have not only served me well, but you have served the people of Annam/ Dai Viet as well and you will accept your reward on my and their behalf. Enough talk from you now. You must also accept fact that you will be considered and treated as an important Mandarin."

Van Ba humbly placed his palms together in front of his face and bowed to Nguyen Hai. "I will accept this honor from you and I will remain your humble servant until I no longer have breath in my body. I know Mot feels the same way. You only need to ask any task of me or her and it will be done to the best of our ability."

"Good! I know your words are truth and your actions always prove your loyalty. The matter is settled. It's time for the dancers so let's watch and have another cup of rice wine. Tonight, we celebrate two great warrior Patriots, you and Mot." After the festivities, everyone had had drank a little too much rice wine, the two groups settled in for the night and fell into a deep and dreamless sleep. The hang overs would come with the morning.

Prior to the wedding day and feast after some tea and bread Van Ba, deep in thought, sat quietly beside Mot, who was waiting for him to speak. When she inquired as to what was troubling him he slowly answered. "Nothing is wrong, things could not be better for us. I can't believe good fortune has come to us. I'm trying to find the best way to tell you of Nguyen Hai's reward for us. When I tell you what it is you probably won't believe me at first. It surprised me and I had trouble believing and accepting it at first, myself."

"Well don't sit there like a dummy, just tell me or I'll do that castration thing and you'll tell me in a high-pitched voice."

"Okay! Okay! I get it! I'll start with the marriage part."

"You'll still be with child at the wedding and will be receiving care from a very good Bac Si until and a short while after the birth. As far as traditional marriage goes we have no family members to visit or dicker over what the dowry will consist of, nor will we have the customary engagement time, or the Hoi.[7] There'll be no lacquered boxes with teas, cakes or fruit to set on the families' ancestral

---

[7]   Betrothal Ceremony.

altars. Nguyen Hai, as our Patron of the No Name and an as Emissary of the Emperor has condoned our marriage and has decried that due to our circumstances some of the Annam/Dai Viet traditions do not apply to us.

"When the wedding day comes he has promised us the most beautiful and lavish Ao Dais to wear, the finest wedding ceremony ever performed, and the biggest and most wonderful feast with the best food, wine and dancers in all of the country performing for us, and to top it off there will be more gifts than we can handle, and envelopes of money in addition to the money he'll bestow upon us. He thinks the feast may last up to three days. Can you imagine that?"

"Van Ba! Are you pulling my leg? I can't believe anyone would ever give something like that to two such unworthy peasant ones as we are."

"I love pulling on your leg for real. Both of them are really nice, but I believe him. I tried not to accept his gifts, but he convinced me that you and I deserved this. If you think this is great let me tell you the rest. You'll have trouble believing it also."

"I guess maybe you are serious after all, so tell me all of it or you may not get to have a leg to pull on."

"I'll save the best for last. At his insistence I must not only get used to being treated more or less like a retired Mandarin, but I have to act like one also, which means you have to act as a Mandarin's Lady does. This means that we will have a most comfortable lifetime together. We'll also have to get used to the people around us looking up to and paying respect to us at all times. It'll be one big change in our humble lives, but I know we will be fair to all. I'll tell you more about being a Mandarin and people farther on."

"Do you remember stories about the ceramic making trade around Van Yen Village in the Chi Linh area close to the Thai Binh River? The rumor is that the area has more than 100 kiln foundations. It is said that the private manor estate of Prince Tran Quoc Tuan, who we all know as Tran Hung Dao, was located there and that the manufacture of the ceramics was a part of it. It faltered because of the loss of trees to kindle the fires used in the production."

"Just outside of the village stands an old estate house. It has about seven rooms, one a kitchen with a fire place for cooking which also opens to the outside if you want to cook there in warmer weather. It's constructed of timber work, wooden posts and walled rooms, (none load bearing), and it is of Chinese architectural painting and decorations, a red glaze roof that is solid with no leaks from the rain. It has a bamboo garden and a small courtyard that is nice. It had belonged to a lesser Mandarin who never married and has passed away."

Interrupting, Mot inquired, "What has that got to do with us?"

"Have patience woman. Oops! Sorry, I mean Mot," he said dodging a kick in the shin. "Well, the property also has six rice paddies and about twenty acres of farm land for planting. There are also workers from the nearby Village who toil there during various planting and harvesting seasons. The estate owner pays them a wage for their efforts. The various rice and vegetables grown there are sold at various markets throughout the Village, its Hamlets, and Sub-Hamlets during the harvesting time. Now you have to guess who owns it."

"Nguyen Hai?"

"No! Try again."

"Does the Invisible One own it?"

"Guess again."

"Van Ba, you are so frustrating. Tell me who right now or I'll start sharpening my knife to do you know what."

"Do you want the truth?"

"I'm warning you," she threatened.

"The newly retired Mandarin and his beautiful Lady are now the new owners!"

"Just who are this new retired Mandarin and his lady?" She thought a minute. "Oh Shit! You said we have to learn how to act differently. You're the new retired Mandarin and I'm his Lady?"

Suddenly she began to jump up and down and spinning around and hollering, "Yes! Van Ba smiled at his bride to be and whispered, "Yes my love. The estate is ours." He grabbed her around the waist, pulled her in to his embrace and kissed her as never before. Then he shouted to the world, "Yes, you are now the Lady of an estate. And don't ever forget, you're my lady too! That is as long as you're the boss." Mot was breathless and speechless for a change and made no attempt to kick a shin.

"Yes!" many times over. Finally, he pulled her to him and spoke calmly into her ear that she needed to calm down as he had more to say. Little by little she slowed down and became less hyper.

"My love, we will have to learn to do numbers. We will have to account for worker's pay, other expenses, keep track of inventory, our sales of product, and also our taxes. You may be better at that than me, but I will always help you with it. Nguyen Hai is going to see that we have enough money to cover our initial expenses for the first few years, plus a little extra, so we don't have to worry about that. I think we will do well, but there is one thing that scares me about the situation."

"I can't believe you'd be afraid of anything except for my sharp knife."

"Remember I commented on the respect of the Villagers and whatnot. My being a retired Mandarin and you a retired

Mandarin's Lady will have the responsibility of holding consultations with single or groups of Villagers or Village Elders, and those from the Hamlets and Sub-Hamlets who come to us for advice. They will expect us to be able to solve their minor or difficult problems. Often it will be difficulties within the family, a neighbor, or a criminal. It could also have to do with the reaping of crops or it could pertain to some crime wave in the area or political nonsense. According to Nguyen Hai it could be anything or everything and we should be prepared for just that. Therefore, we will have to learn all we can about the village its people, and its history and even develop individuals to keep us secretly informed of the goings on in the various areas. That does scare me a little because it's so different from the harsh life we've lived up to now. I'm not a man of learning or one who never gave learning a thought.

"I'm glad you mentioned this to me now. We can prepare ourselves for this and I know we will do quite well at it. You will be a great retired Mandarin. Of course, I'll be coaching you all the way. Now, it's time for me to discuss something with you that Nguyen Hai related to me on the way from the feast. I'm not comfortable at all with parts of it, however I accept it as is our Vietnamese custom."

Mot continued with her explanation. "We will have a live in house keeper to do the cooking, serving, cleaning, and to watch the children on occasion. That is the first thing. He had mentioned several servants but I said no. Next, you are going to be an important person, he didn't say you would be a Mandarin, I'm surprised at that, and that you will be expected to act in the way of an important man. He did say there are times when an important man needs to be satisfied by a woman and his wife, due to that time of month or child birth, illness or whatever, cannot satisfy his needs. The man is expected to have one or more concubines or someone around who can satisfy him temporarily. I knew about this custom and although I'm not really happy about it, I agreed with it, but told him that I knew you would not be willing to have any concubine. I also told him that no way would I want some sweet young thing around you, especially with your sex drive. He did have a solution to the problem and one that I most likely can agree to and live with.

"He didn't say anything about that to me Mot. You're right that in thinking that I don't want a concubine. I've never been one to be a cheater. Not on my past wife or any woman I might have been seeing at the time. I want you! Not a concubine. So, what is this solution he has proposed?"

"He promised me that he would not put some young sexy thing in the house that would want you and compete with me for your' affection. However, the house keeper will take care of you when it's needed and sometimes extra if you want. I'm sure you will need extra at times. You may know her. In fact, I know you do know her."

"How in the world would I know a house keeper? I've never had any place that needed a house keeper. I don't make messes any way, I take care of myself."

"Nguyen Hai sent a messenger to her sub-hamlet to ask her if she would be willing to do the chores and service you when needed and she replied that she would be honored to accept on your behalf. I'd bet you it would be on her behalf too!"

"Who, I might ask, 'is the solution to this problem?' I can't believe I could possibly know anyone who would take on this kind of responsibility, especially of servicing me when its needed."

"This will greatly surprise you, my lover. You do know her very well. She is from your own sub hamlet, your woman friend and past consort, Nguyen Thi Tranh."

"Surely you're joking. It's Tranh?"

"I'm serious about this. It will be her. From what Nguyen Hai told me she has taken care of you on many occasions and would be honored to serve you in your house hold needs, serve your' family, and any time you're in need of sexual satisfaction she'd be there for you. I feel confident that she is a good person from what he said to me, she's a very hard worker, one who likes and highly respects you and will not try to take advantage of us. Although I don't agree about you getting satisfied with anyone else I'm glad she is someone who will want to comfort you when you are in need, and I know in my heart that I want you to always be a satisfied man. If you take advantage of it though, just remember this, I still have a sharp knife and know how to use it."

"Mot, I don't know what to say. I don't want anyone else but you. There are many things we do together that will satisfy me. I need to tell you this. After my wife died I had a woman from time to time in different places I happened to be in, but they were not someone to love or stay with, let alone marry them. After moving to my present sub-hamlet, I met Tranh. After knowing her a while, she asked me to repair her table. I obliged her, and did the best I could with the old table. She thanked me by cooking me supper. She proved that she is a good cook and also her place was very clean. I had nothing else to do after eating so I sat with her and we talked. From out of nowhere she said that she had had no man in a long while and wouldn't mind being with one every once in a while. She told me that she liked me more than other men in the area and wouldn't be opposed to my taking all of her. I told her I kind of liked her too. I was horny and so was she."

"That's how it started with us. We were on and off. I'd be with her a day or two or she with me a day or two, then it could be a few weeks before we'd get together again because I'd be on a mission for the No Name. I'll be as honest as I can about this. I liked her more than others I had had. She was very soothing, comforting and I enjoyed her sex. As nice as she is, sex was with her it was nothing like what you and I have together. I liked and respected her, but was not in love with her. You're magnificent my love. If I really have to do it to satisfy myself with someone, she is the only one other than you that I would ever consider doing anything with."

"Oh Van Ba, I'm glad you told me this. It makes me a little more comfortable thinking about it. I won't have to worry about you straying far from my nest. I think right now, speaking about my nest, I need you to be a bird with a long beak and enter my nest." He did.

The Marriage Ceremony and the feasting that lasted three days, which was attended by several Mandarins and high-level people of the No Name, was over, and the newlyweds moved into their estate home. Tranh was already there and had a delicious lunch meal prepared for them. Before serving her new employers Van Ba introduced her to Mot. The two women hugged and looked at each other kindly. Mot let her know that they had a lot to talk about and they would sit in the garden by the courtyard later. She also told her that unless there were important people visiting she needn't be formal as employees were normally mandated to be. After their lunch was over the two women went to the bamboo garden and talked, some about her duties, mostly about Van Ba and what was in the past and what happens in the future between Tranh and him, when needed, was okay with her.

Mot also thanked her for being willing to be their employee under the circumstances. Tranh accepted her thanks, spoke of this being a chance for her to have a better life, and assured her that she will be dedicated to the family and promised faithfully she would only service Van Ba only if she received permission from Mot. Mot replied, "I think I'll leave that decision to Van Ba and you to make. I'll make sure he's so horny sometimes that he'll come to you for extra understanding and comfort. Maybe I'll even get him to crawl on his knees by threatening him with my knife to his family jewels." They both laughed and hugged.

The years went by and their farming and sales were very profitable for them. The villagers worshiped them as they were kind, receptive, and helpful in solving problems for them. Mot had birthed three baby boys into the family. Van Ba taught them rice and vegetable growing and harvesting while Mot taught them manners, martial arts and how to operate the business. The boys, having grown into strong handsome men, some said their looks came from their mother, they married and moved into their own homes close by with a small piece of land of their own, part of the estate given to them by Van Ba and Mot. Their understanding, with their parents was that upon the parents' deaths the first born would inherit the estate, be the new Mandarin, the second one would run the business, and the third would supervise the planting and harvesting and sales. The fact that the boys still helped with those tasks meant they would be familiar with and ready to accept the responsibilities that they would inherit.

Van Ba soon became accustomed to the agreement with Tranh. At first he was tentative about the sex with Tranh because of his feelings towards Mot. They were still good together, but they didn't push the limits. Within a few months she was becoming a part of the family. During all three of her pregnancies Mot would have to refrain from sex from time to time and she was content to know that her man was being cared for by someone who cared about him nearly as much as she did. Tranh also became invaluable in the caring and training of the infants over the years as Mot had a hard time delivering all three and needed to rest longer than most new mothers. As the boys grew they became very fond of Tranh and she was the closest thing to a grandmother they had.

When the oldest boy was fifteen years old Tranh, who had become sickly a few years before, passed away, and Mot took over the duties of cooking and the upkeep of the house. Van Ba was beginning to show his age, but they still made passionate love their pastime. Their love seemed to become stronger the more they aged.

Nguyen Hai, until recently had visited often and had also aged and handed the reins of the No Name to the Invisible One, then shortly passed away. Young Da, on becoming a fierce fighter and better at the game of being a great warrior, became the new Invisible One for the No Name. The two of them would visit the estate whenever possible, bringing along their' wives. During the visits the tales of their feats became longer and more heroic with each and every telling. Sometimes they would tell their heroic tales at the Village feasts held after harvest time. The Villagers worshiped all the Heroes and always looked forward to the great feats of the story telling.

Throughout the years every morning Van Ba and Mot would rise just before sunup, make a little love, until they couldn't due to their ages, and before workers got to the fields. They would walk around some of the property, enjoying the early morning sunrise cast it's rays over their' domain, even in the cold of the monsoon season. They would stroll along hand in hand, sometimes stopping for a hug and a kiss, and each was still thankful for the other.

The time came eventually when Van Ba's body began failing him. His legs had lost some of their strength and he needed to walk slower and with a walking stick as he now staggered a lot. Mot was getting older too, but since she was a little younger than he, she still had most of her strength. As time crept on Mot began to age more also, but she could still help Van Ba along during their morning walks. Eventually, their walks over their domain became shorter and shorter as they both aged more and became weaker and the walks were now sometimes becoming a struggle for both.

One misty morning, a paddy worker came to work a little earlier than usual because he wanted to ask a favor of Van Ba and Mot that he was sure would be granted to him. He went to the house, knocked on the door, called out, and no one answered the knock or call. He went to the bamboo garden and the courtyard, but no one was there either. He then presumed that the couple was still on their morning walk and maybe they needed help as some mornings they were very lucky to make it back to the house.

He then went to check the rice paddy area as it was the closest area to the house to see if they needed any help. Approaching the first paddy, he saw two people lying down close to the first dyke. As he approached the two he saw that it was the bodies of Van Ba and Mot. They had passed away together and were laying side by side, still holding hands with each other. He cried and wailed wildly and ran to the eldest son's home.

JADE CROSS TRILOGY

BEFORE THE JADE CROSS EVENT

A MALEVELENT BOOK 2
COMING SOON

BOOK 2 OF THE JADE CROSS TRILOGY will be available shortly. It introduces the main characters of the JADE CROSS, Book 3, the final book of the trilogy.

The book takes Marine Retired Master Gunnery Sergeant Travis Tolbane and his Marine Corps Buddy, Detective Jim Parnell, no longer on active duty, of the Nashville Metropolitan Police Department, through some facets of retail security, and the antagonist who hates Tolbane from apprehending him during the commission of a crime while serving at the Chu Lai Combat Base in the Republic of South Viet Nam in 1966.

Read the Chapter "1965," now and later the novel to delve into some convoluted events after Tolbane retired from the U. S. Marine Corps after 30 years.

A love story, crime, murder, a malevolent piquerist and his paramour, the Book 2 story has it all.

1965

REPUBLIC OF VIETNAM

It was late November of 1965. SSgt Travis Tolbane was uncomfortable on the fold down bench, pipe frame seats and backs with cloth strips crises crossed and stretched between the pipes, as the aircraft hit a small area of light turbulence causing minor vibrating of the craft. He was turned slightly to his right with his knees against a huge packing crate, somewhere over the Pacific Ocean between MCAS Futenma, Okinawa and Da Nang, Quang Nam Provence, Republic of Viet Nam. The whole center of the C 130 Cargo plane was loaded with huge crates, piled a little higher than his head and extended nearly to the seating area on each side of them, bound for the war zone in the Republic of Viet Nam. He was not alone in his discomfort.

Marines he didn't know were seated along both sides of the interior of the craft and were as cramped up as he. The thing that puzzled him was that most troops were being transported by jet passenger aircraft or by the sea for whole units to the conflict zone; why not him. He was feeling it strange too that this craft left from MCAS Futenma. He had been with Marine Air Group 16, First Marine

Air Wing, a helicopter unit, when it moved from the old WWII era hospital, Camp Mercy, to the newly constructed Air Station in 1960. He had flown in choppers many times, but never in a prop driven C 130 transport loaded to its capacity droning along. He wondered how in the hell did he end up in this cramped situation in what seemed to be a lumbering air plane, half scaring the crap out of hm.

After he graduated from boot camp, he went through Advanced Combat Training at the 1st Infantry Training Regiment (ITR) at Camp Geiger, Camp Lejune NC. Serving 30 days mess duty to start and then when the training cycle was complete the newly promoted PFC found himself sitting in front of a Gunny Sgt. in the Regimental Hq. The Gunny informed him his MOS had been changed from Infantry to clerical as two clerks had been transferred out and they were in need of fresh blood. While clerking at ITR he learned to type and the ins and outs of Marine Corps Procedure Manuals, the Landing Party Manual, NAV. MCs. and others, and developed various methods of helping fellow Marines with their administrative problems. He excelled in his tasks and received two meritorious promotions before his transfer to Okinawa.

When he rotated back to the states, he was now an E-5 Sgt. He was tired of clerical work and took a Foreign Language Aptitude Test and scored higher than the average individual. When informed of his passing the test he was required to fill out a form indicating what three languages he preferred to study. He found himself attending the US Army Language School, which later became the Defense Language Institute, West Coast Branch, in the Middle Eastern Language Division studying the Arabic Language, so much for wanting to learn German, Spanish or French.

A Year later he was on the Second Composite Interrogation Team at Camp Lejune, NC, which later became the 2nd, 4th, and 6th teams. Until he received orders to Viet Nam, he had kept himself immersed in Middle Eastern history and present affairs and even had a temporary assignment in Morocco. He made Staff Sgt. the first time he was eligible.

Nearly six hours after takeoff they were on the final approach to the Da Nang air strip. Over the intercom they were informed by the pilot to fasten their seatbelts as well as a possibility of sniper fire hitting the plane on the approach and landing. On touch down they were to grab their gear and when the ramp was lowered, by a crewman, to get off the plane as quickly as possible and run hell bent to the Terminal building if they wanted to keep from getting dinged with a lucky shot from some Victor Charley sniping at them from afar, and line up at the Marine New Arrivals counter, have a copy of their orders in hand to check in and get their unit assignments and transportation instructions.

This made Tolbane wonder even more about what he had gotten into. It wasn't the run to the building or the carrying of gear that got to him. It was the god-awful heat and mugginess that hit him and the others when the ramp came down. He did feel better though when he felt he was safe in the terminal building even though it was hot and muggy in there too. There was some confusion with the Marines digging out a copy of their orders they had stashed in their gear to start with and then they were in line to hurry up and wait, behind an empty counter, and to wait was the Marine Corps standard procedure.

After checking in those going to units outside of the Da Nang area were told where to wait for pickups outside of the terminal. The rest, including Tolbane, were sent to a tent area, a few GP (General Purpose tents), with folding cots where they would receive their 'In Country Orientation and Briefings' to prepare them for their tour. It became basically classes on what not to do or get your butt kicked out of country and how it would affect their military careers. This was on his second day there and after the Orientation he sat around in the tent, sweating to extreme even though the tent sides were rolled up, except going to chow, until midday of the third day. Then a jeep pulled up to the tent and Tolbane met one of his future team mates was told to grab his gear and climb aboard, and was transported to his Team's Command Post.

He had a little problem in the beginning of his tour adjusting to the questioning of prisoners as he had no knowledge at all of not only Vietnamese Culture the Army of the Republic of Viet Nam, Popular forces and the Viet Cong, and etc., but exactly what was really happening in the skirmishes the troops were having, the terrain, the location of the various hamlets, sub-hamlets, and the actual way the people lived, worked and how they were caught up between the two sides of the conflict. The fact that the military maps weren't totally accurate didn't help any either. He worked hard to ply his trade working with and questioning various Vietnamese Army Interpreters assigned to his team he learned a lot about the Vietnamese History and their' traditions. The one thing he was really surprised at was the fact that they were testing the use of a polygraph operator on certain VCS/VCC (Viet Cong Confirmed/Viet Cong Suspects).

Soon he was finding himself feeling confident in his ability, especially when working with an interpreter named Ba. A month and a half after arriving in Da Nang he was assigned to one of the Teams Sub-Teams assigned to the Seventh Marines at the Chu Lai Combat Base; Ba was sent with him. The Sub Team's CP was a tent at the MP's Captive Collection Point just off the end of the runway and hard back tents on top of what seemed to be a sand dune, was their billeting area overlooking the China Sea coast line and parts of the combat base.

He and Ba had great success in their endeavors there. He worked well with the Regimental S2 Shop while being on several operations with the Seventh Marines down in Quang Ngai Provence, close to Quang Ngai City. It wasn't long until the Intelligence Officer was asking for Tolbane and BA rather than one of the other interrogators, depended on Tolbane and Ba's extraction of vital information on the operations from Viet Cong Suspects and those Confirmed as Viet Cong as well as interviewing the local people.

It had been a few months since he had wondered what the hell he was doing there. Having a work ethic was not a problem with him. He had always dedicated himself to his work since boot camp where you were immersed from before dawn as in O Dark Thirty Hours to Taps at 2200 hrs. His major concern was when being transported to and from Quang Ngai Provence in two and a half ton trucks and whether or not they would be ambushed by the enemy. So far only a couple of trucks had hit land mines. As fortune would have it the vehicles were empty of troops and the drivers and their assistant drivers only received minor wounds because a rear tire had hit the mine. For the first time he saw for the UH1 Huey helicopter gunships. His only experiences with helicopters was the UH 34s of MAG 16. The UH1s were buzzing around overhead for their protection while the convoy was held up. He had had no idea they were even there before the rear of the truck hit the mine

When the next Staff NCO promotion list came out Tolbane found he was promoted to Gunnery Sgt. All of his team except himself, Ba, a Corporeal and his Interpreter had returned to their Da Nang CP leaving them alone in their compound. Sometime in late May he and Ba returned to Da Nang, their Temporary Assigned Duty had been terminated, as the First Marine Division Headquarters had arrived in March and now had their own Interrogation Translation Team which Tolbane had helped orient and train in the art of Interrogation, as well as the current situation, including sociological makeup of the people and the geography of the area. The new Team was fresh out of a six-month Vietnamese course at Language School and had no prior Intelligence training knew as much about Viet Nam as he had known on his arrival in country.

His Promotion Warrant was waiting for him on his arrival. After receiving it he and the other Team Staff NCOs grabbed the team's jeeps and went to the Army's 'Take Ten Club' in Da Nang for His 'Wetting Down' party. Of course, he had to foot the bill as being the celeb of the party and receive the 'Tacking On' of his new rank by Senior Staff NCOs, which consisted of being punched on each upper arm by each of the others as hard as they could leaving one with sore bicep muscles and bruises for a day or two, or three, such was another great Marine Corps Tradition. He was poured into one of the jeeps when the "Wetting Down' was over and taken back to the Team CP and tossed onto his cot.